Dave's Eyes
Were Dreamy with Passion

He let his hands slide to her waist, pulling her close against him. "Do you really want to go home, Ellen? You can stay and be here early for rehearsal..." His lips were brushing against her hair, teasing and taunting her. When his hands moved to her well rounded backside, pulling her hips tight against him, she pushed away. Damn! She wanted him! It would be so easy. With one little word she could have him— for tonight, at least. One night, then she could return to her resolution, just one night of ecstasy....

Dear Reader:

We've had thousands of wonderful surprises at SECOND CHANCE AT LOVE since we launched the line in June 1981.

We knew we were going to have to work hard to bring you the six best romances we could each month. We knew we were working with a talented, caring group of authors. But we *didn't* know we were going to receive such a warm and generous response from readers. So the thousands of wonderful surprises are in the form of letters from readers like you who've been kind with your praise, constructive and helpful with your suggestions. We read each letter...and take it seriously.

It's been a thrill to "meet" our readers, to discover that the people who read SECOND CHANCE AT LOVE novels and write to us about them are so remarkable. Our romances can only get better and better as we learn more and more about you, the reader, and what you like to read.

So, I hope you will continue to enjoy SECOND CHANCE AT LOVE and, if you haven't written to us before, please feel free to do so. If you have written, keep in touch.

With every good wish,

Sincerely,

Carolyn Nichols

Carolyn Nichols
SECOND CHANCE AT LOVE
The Berkley/Jove Publishing Group
200 Madison Avenue
New York, New York 10016

P.S. Because your opinions *are* so important to us, I urge you to fill out and return the questionnaire in the back of this book.

STARBURST
TESS EWING

A SECOND CHANCE AT LOVE BOOK

Chapter One

ELLEN MCKAY EASED her trim, size-six body behind the wheel of her aging blue Malibu Classic. She was exhausted from the audition she had just suffered through, and now that it was over, she felt limp, completely drained of all emotion and energy. It was impossible to tell if Dave Winston had considered her a serious contender for the spot of backup singer in his group. He had remained stony, seated unmoving at the table in the audition room, throughout the lengthy tryouts. There was no way she could read an expression on his handsome face or detect a single response in his velvety brown eyes.

She felt around in the bottom of her tote bag for something to tie back her shoulder-length auburn hair. A rubber band did the trick, making her feel cooler in the Nashville heat. With a sigh, she turned the key in the ignition; briefly the motor sputtered and moaned, then reluctantly purred to life.

"Nice baby." She reached out to pat the dashboard. "I know you're terminal, and I feel sorry for you, but just hang in there a little longer...*please!*" The ailing Malibu was one of her worries, now that her short gig at the Hay Barn, on the outskirts of Nashville, had come to an abrupt end.

"No more money to pay singers," the boss man had said, and that was the end of that, her singing job with the third-rate "Cowhands." It sure had been a whole lot better than nothing, she thought ruefully. It had allowed her to live in the manner to which she was accustomed— one step above the poverty level. She smiled to herself. But she definitely wanted something better. At the moment, though, just a job would do, because, unfortunately, she had to pay the rent on her apartment and eat now and then. Alimony had not been a part of her divorce decree. She didn't want anything from Carl.

She sighed. Dave Winston's manager had said, "We'll let you gals know as soon as we can who gets the job." Sure, they would, but when?

After spending five years of her life, including the disastrous years of marriage to Carl, taking any honky-tonk job she could find, she should be well aware of the facts of life in Music City.

She strummed her short, well-manicured fingers on the steering wheel as if it were her old guitar, while she waited to turn out of the parking lot onto the main street. Broke now, she thought. Broke then. Always broke. She wrinkled her nose and, catching her reflection in the rearview mirror, stuck out her tongue at herself.

Actually, the marriage hadn't been bad at first. They

had had fun. Just being together was enough for them then.

"It doesn't take money to make love, angel," Carl used to tell her. "When we get to the top we'll do it on satin sheets." She had never felt those sheets. Unfortunately, when the breaks did come for Carl and he started his steady climb up the ladder of fame, they began to drift apart. The female fans discovered Carl, and Carl discovered he had a very active roving eye. It was only a matter of time until he began to roam. Ellen remembered how humiliated and bitter she'd felt and how she'd hung on for a whole year, hating to admit it was over between them, that she'd made an awful mistake.

She eased her car into the line of traffic, her gray-green eyes narrowing as she headed into the bright sun. It had taken time to pull her life together, to put herself in control of her destiny once again, to regain some of the sense of humor of her earlier years. There were no longer any tears, and only occasionally a jag of self-pity.

The backup singer job with Dave Winston and his group, the Greyhounds, which she had been steered to by her agent, Mack Donner, could be the start she needed. It wasn't much—no solo work, strictly chorus stuff and harmony with three others, two men and another woman. But it would get her out of the dingy honky-tonks and into where the action was. She would be seen on stage with Dave Winston, whose name was spelled in big neon lights on marquees across the country. After that, *anything* could happen. But she didn't dare hope too much. So many singers had auditioned for that spot with him.

She hummed a few bars of one of his ballads, conjuring up a mental picture she cherished. Ellen Kern—no, she was Ellen McKay again . . . she kept forgetting—

was a star, on stage at the Grand Ole Opry, wearing a skintight red Western outfit, waving her white cowgirl hat as she bowed to thunderous applause.

The van ahead of her squealed to a stop as the signal light at the intersection changed to red. Ellen slammed down hard on her own brakes, hoping the red sports car behind her would stop in time. All she needed was an accident! "Better put aside your daydreaming, Ellen Patricia," she muttered, "or you won't have to worry about paying the rent, making it at the Opry . . . or anything else."

She glanced at her watch. No wonder her stomach was beginning to growl. She hadn't had anything to eat since breakfast, and it was almost six o'clock. "Wow!" She expelled her breath sharply. Dave Winston sure had taken his sweet time with those auditions.

She turned left when the signal changed, anxious to get home. In the rearview mirror she saw the shiny red car turn the corner and move up to tailgate her Malibu. "Idiot," she hissed at the reflected image. "You and your expensive piece of horsepower ought to go back to drivers'-training class."

She felt more her fresh-talking old self then, and when she glanced at the fast-food places dotting the sides of the road ahead, made a hasty decision. She patted her stomach. "Pizza for you, empty friend. The pitiful budget will just about stretch to that little treat." She swung into the Pizza Port parking lot, her eyes automatically going again to the rearview mirror. The red car—a Mercedes, she noted—spun into the lot, right on her tail still, and pulled into the parking space next to hers. Ellen was tempted to look over at the driver, but she kept her eyes down, pretending to rummage in her purse. It was, after all, merely a coincidence that the car had been behind her for several miles. Or was it? She bit her lip, scowling, then quickly rolled up the window and locked the door. Come to think of it, that car had been visible in her rearview mirror since she left the audition. There was a tapping sound on her window, and she almost jumped halfway across the front seat. She took a deep breath and turned slowly.

A tall, dark, decidedly handsome Dave Winston was a mere thickness of glass away! He made a cranking motion, and she quickly rolled down her window.

"Hello, Ellen." His smile started sensations stirring in her lower anatomy that had nothing to do with hunger.

"Look, I rarely bite," he said. "You're staring at me like I'm Dracula." He bared his teeth and laughed, his dark eyes coming alive with fire-building sparks.

Ellen grinned. "And I'm Vampira, buster, starving to death, so watch out!" She bared her teeth as he had, and they both laughed.

Dave reached in and pulled up the lock, then opened the door. "Safest thing is for us to attack a thick, gooey pizza and a pitcher of beer, not each other. Don't you think?" He winked and drew her out of the car. "I *am* a monster for keeping you and all those other gals around that audition room for so many hours."

"A true ogre," she shot back. He was talking to her so casually, like it was an everyday thing, and he was standing so close! Suddenly his nearness turned her legs to sponge. Crazy, she told herself. She had just shaken free from one conceited male. What the hell was she doing responding like a gawky girl to *this* one?

Dave led her to the restaurant, pausing before they pushed through the glass doors and taking a pair of heavily-tinted glasses from the pocket of his navy-blue jacket. "Occupational hazard," he told her, putting them on.

"It's difficult to enjoy a meal in peace. The good thing is fans don't expect to see me eating in a place like this. Let me pick the table, OK?"

She shrugged. "Fine." And briefly, she wondered if she would ever have a problem dodging fans. Right now it sounded great.

Fortunately, there was only a handful of customers in the tiny eating place, and no one even seemed to notice them as they ordered their pizza and beer and went to a corner table. Dave removed the dark glasses and stuffed them back into the pocket of his jacket. "I guess I won't need these after all. That's good. I want to be able to see you when I give you the good news."

She swallowed, trying to look indifferent. "What good news, Mr. Winston?"

His sun-bronzed hand grasped hers and held it firmly. Her instantaneous excitement angered her. Not since she and Carl had been dating, so in love they couldn't keep their hands off each other, had a man affected her as Dave Winston was affecting her at this moment. She tugged her hand, but Dave held it tighter for a second before releasing it.

"First of all, if we're going to be working together, you had better get used to calling me Dave."

She nodded, dazedly aware of his words. "Dave . . ."

His laugh was musical. "Oh, you're something else. Did you hear what I just said, Ellen McKay? You are my new backup singer. You can start right away, tomorrow morning, at rehearsal at my place. I have a studio there. What do you think?"

"What do I think?" she whooped, then went suddenly limp. "You aren't kidding me, are you?"

"No joke here and no contest back there. Wasn't a singer in that room had anything on you, hon. You've got a style that's fresh as a buttercup and a sound that's sweet and clear as dew."

"Oh, Mr. Winston . . . Dave . . . I . . ." She couldn't find a single word. Rich laughter poured out, expressing better than words her pure pleasure at getting the job—and hearing his praise.

He winked at her. "Didn't you know you made every other gal at the audition look and sound like she'd been around the barn more times than you'd even looked at it?"

"Now, wait a sec," she said, still grinning, but crinkling her brow in suspicion. "If I was such a gosh-darned sure thing, why did you make me and everybody else try out the good Lord only knows how many times alone and in twos and threes?"

"Why, Ellen McKay!" His eyes gleamed with mischief. "Now, you wouldn't think I'd do a mean, low-down thing like feed you a line, would you?"

"A line? Why, no, sir. Maybe just slather on the cream a little too thick for me to swallow?"

He hooted and reached out to squeeze her fingers. "Didn't I have to cover myself? After all, even now you haven't said yes to joining me and the Greyhounds." He shrugged. "What if you turn me down flat? Got to have a list of contenders so I'll come out getting some backup singer, even if she's not the best."

"So everyone had to sweat—starve!—and hope while you ranked us all from one to twenty, huh?" She was starry-eyed and bantering, but there was a tinge of real criticism to her words.

"Why, you sassy . . ." Dave's teasing voice died, and his bright brown eyes went soft and serious. "You know, I didn't look at today from the right angle at all. I forgot how it feels to be wanting a break and needing a job.

Damn," he said huskily. "I must be getting too big for my britches. I was just thinking about me and mine." He paused, staring thoughtfully at her. "You know," he murmured, "I think you're going to be real good for me and the Greyhounds in more ways—"

A sudden squeal interrupted him. "You're Dave Winston!" The waitress slid the pizza in front of them, almost dropping it in Dave's lap.

He nodded, his eyes twinkling. "I think so. At least, I was when I left home this morning. It *has* been a busy day, though. I might have lost old Dave in the shuffle."

The girl giggled, so obviously flustered that Ellen felt a pang of pity for her. The young Dave Winston fan raved on. "You know what I mean. Oh, I'm just so excited to see you right here in *my* restaurant." Again the giggle. "I mean...here where I work...I mean, I don't really own the place."

She fumbled in the pocket of her blue uniform and brought out her order pad and pencil. "Would you sign this for me? I'd sure appreciate it. I have to tell you you're my favorite country-western singer. I just bought your new *Hello to Love* album yesterday."

Ellen watched the girl's animated face. "Enthralled" was the word for her expression. She was in seventh heaven to be talking to her hero. Would anyone ever look at her that way, be willing to practically die in a crowd for her autograph? It must be a thrill. No wonder Carl had lost his values and let his head inflate with a sense of importance. Probably Dave Winston was the same way. How could he help but be, with girls swarming after him constantly, adoring him, offering themselves to him? She shuddered and poured herself a glass of beer while Dave obligingly signed his name on the pad the waitress shoved at him.

He handed it back, and she dropped it in the middle of the pizza, retrieving it hastily and wiping it off on her apron. "Thanks so much." She backed away, glancing briefly at Ellen to see if she was worth wasting a sheet of paper on. Ellen smiled to herself and then wondered if the young woman was envying her because she was with Dave. She had gone through that, too, with Carl. There wasn't much future, being in love with a star.

"Sorry about the interruption, Ellen."

"No need to apologize, Mr. Winston. Why, I'm just so thrilled to be sitting here with you I don't know what to do!" She imitated the waitress's giggly, excited voice, and Dave laughed.

"I like you, Ellen McKay. I think I'd enjoy making your name a household word. How about that?"

Ellen sliced into the pizza and pulled off a gooey slice. Her eyes slanted to meet his. "It sounds wonderful. Why do I have the feeling there will be some very tiny print in the contract?" She bit off a mouthful of the pizza, savoring the spicy flavor, but knowing, too, she was eating in a playfully provocative way.

Dave filled his mug from the glass pitcher and cut himself a piece of the still-steaming pizza. "No fine print. Honest. I read on your application that you've been trying for a long time. Let's say you remind me of my kid sister. I'd want someone to give her a break."

"Oh?" Her eyebrows rose. "Do you have a sister?"

He shook his head, his dark eyes twinkling. "No. But, if I *did,* I think I'd want her to be just like you." He shrugged, taking time to enjoy the pizza before adding, "OK. Call it instant intuition. I happen to think you have talent. Sometimes living here in Music City doesn't help. It isn't easy to get a break."

Ellen nodded. "Don't I know it. My ex-husband and

I knocked on every door in town a dozen times a month. I guess you could say I already have a name for myself in Nashville." She laughed. "No one remembers it, though." He was watching her intently, and she felt uneasy. "I was married to Carl Kern," she informed him.

"Oh, sure. He's doing great things on the West Coast now, I hear."

"H-m-m, great," she echoed noncommittally.

"Well," Dave said, a crooked grin on his handsome face, "is it yes to the job or are you gonna say no to me?"

Again their eyes met, and held. Say no to him? Impossible, Ellen thought, impossible to say no to anything he asked this minute. She felt fire smolder inside her. It was a feeling she hadn't experienced in a very long time. Heaven help her—right at the moment, she wanted Dave Winston... wanted to leave this tiny public place and go somewhere private where he could hold her in those strong-looking arms of his. She wanted to feel that sensuous mouth close over hers and his hands caress her body. As if reading her thoughts, Dave reached out to gain possession of her hand, and he raised it to his mouth, letting his lips brush across her fingers and sending a tingling sensation up her arm.

"Of course I'm going to say yes," she murmured, but to her own ears the words sounded strange, as if she were answering the wrong question. Quickly she stammered a correction. "I mean... that is... well, who could turn down a chance to be one of Dave Winston's singers?"

He merely smiled and went on staring in that hypnotizing way.

"Let's drive out to my place on the lake and talk about the job," he said at last, breaking the spell. "Maybe we can go over some of the songs we do, get the feel of them before rehearsal tomorrow morning."

"Tomorrow morning?" She came back to the present, although his breath on her fingertips was very disconcerting. A warning flashed in her mind. "Lordy Lou," her inner self exclaimed, "you know exactly what he's up to and you don't care." But common sense came to the rescue and told her to refuse his invitation, because this game might prove a little dangerous. And just this once she let common sense reign.

"I'm sorry, Dave. I . . . I really can't make it tonight. Would it be all right if I start rehearsing with you and the group tomorrow?" She didn't have to offer any explanation. After all, she didn't know him well enough to owe one, yet still she watched his face intently for any sign of annoyance.

With a shake of his head, he put her hand down on the table, patted it once, big-brother fashion, and poured himself another glass of brew. "Sure . . . if you prefer it that way. Tomorrow will be just fine."

"Oh, *just* fine?" she repeated, disappointment at his swift acquiescence making her tone sarcastic. She felt as deflated as an old swim float tossed into the attic for the wintertime. "I thought it was real important to get a jump start on the rehearsals with the whole group."

"Wouldn't want to put you out, though." There was a mocking, challenging gleam in his eyes.

Chapter Two

SUDDENLY ELLEN FELT very reckless. Why shouldn't she go? She was a big girl now, and certainly ought to be able to handle him, her tangled emotions, and some singing, too.

She shrugged. "Well, I guess I could change my plans for one evening. It would be better for the group if I went over the songs ahead of time." She smiled at the way his face brightened, like a little boy just given a candied apple.

He flashed her an infectious grin. "Great. I don't live far from here, just a few miles out in the boondocks. I like it private." He drained his mug of beer and thumped it on the table. "We all get together three or four times a week at the studio to practice. If we're doing new songs, we practically live out there. My housekeeper,

Aggie, brings meals to us in the studio, and we work far into the night. I think you'll like the gang, Ellen. Tom and Janet Adams are newlyweds. They met on my show a year ago and had a real whirlwind romance. Chuck and Lynn share an apartment in the city. The scuttlebutt has it they're planning a big wedding right after their offspring is born. Lynn is the perky little gal you're replacing. She's plenty modern about some things, but she insists on staying home to take care of the baby for a few months before going back to work."

Ellen nodded. "I'd probably do the same." She paused, watching his face. "So if everything works out, I can stay on the job for as long as Lynn's gone, right?"

"You've got it." He winked at her, then nodded toward the door. "Come on, let's hit the road."

Ellen gobbled her last bite of pizza, swallowed a mouthful of beer, wiped her fingers and mouth on a napkin and pushed back her chair. "OK, I'm ready. Lead on, MacWinston."

Dave walked close, and she felt a rush of heat at his nearness. The girl behind the counter called, "Goodbye, Dave. Come on back soon, you hear?" Her drawl gave way to a giggling farewell, bringing Ellen quickly back to earth.

"See you, honey," Dave told the girl, and Ellen knew his words must have sent the waitress into orbit, sparks flying. She'd surely tell everyone who came into the Pizza Port that *the* Dave Winston had called her honey. Ellen sighed. She could understand the girl's feelings. She wasn't far from orbit herself, and the sparks were definitely flying.

When they reached the parking lot, Dave turned her to face him. "What's so funny?" His brow wrinkled into a frown. "That smile of yours is real mysterious and making me nuts."

She laughed aloud, relieving her tension. "Nothing is really funny. I was just tickled at how thrilled that waitress was when you called her honey. You made her day, you know."

Without warning he reached out and tilted her head back, planting a warm kiss directly on target. Her lips tingled with pleasure, and she fought the urge to wind her arms around his neck and not let the kisses stop. When Dave stepped back, she felt a twinge of disappointment.

"And how about you? Did that thrill you, *honey?*" His eyes danced, forcing her to respond with a smile.

"Oh, yes, dear, clear to the soles of my sandals." She wasn't about to inform him that the meeting of their lips had indeed made her heart thump hard. She moved quickly to her car. "I'll follow you, right?"

"Wrong." He reached over to take her arm in a firm grasp. "There's no sense taking two cars and using twice as much gas. I'll drive, then bring you back here for your car when you're ready. Fair enough? We can talk on the way to my place."

"Greyhound Acres?"

"Guess almost everybody around Nashville knows it, huh? Ten acres of good country land. Named the place after my racing greyhounds. Got a pair of beauts I'm real crazy about, and hope to have a litter of little winners any day—whenever Mrs. Grey decides to deliver." He gazed down at her. "We sure have a lot of getting acquainted to do."

She smiled as he opened the car door for her. He was on his good behavior, no doubt. She wondered when the real Dave Winston would burst forth and what he would be like. Well, two could play at the politeness game. She reached across and unlocked his door. When he slid in beside her, she turned to face him, studying his finely chiseled features a moment before speaking. "You surprise me. I never would have guessed a big-time recording star like Dave Winston would be interested in raising dogs."

He flashed her a cocky grin, designed to make any woman swoon. "Stick with me, honey. You just might have a few more surprises in store for you."

"I'll bet!" She opened her clutch purse and took out a pack of cigarettes. "Mind if I smoke?"

He shook his head, glancing at her, puzzled. "If you're addicted to the weed, how come you didn't light up at the Pizza Port?"

Ellen shrugged, pushed in the car cigarette lighter, and waited for it to pop back out, then touched it to the end of her cigarette. She took a long drag, exhaling slowly. "I'm trying to cut down, but it isn't easy. I never smoked at all until I met Carl. He was a human chimney—never stopped spewing smoke." A half-smile tugged at her sensuous mouth. She sighed. "I smoke now when I'm nervous."

As soon as the words left her mouth, she wished she could recall them. Dave chuckled and pushed his shiny black Western boot down on the gas pedal. The Mercedes lunged ahead to roar down the open highway, away from the city, its engine vibrating with power still held in check.

"I hope I don't make you nervous. I swear, ma'am, I'm harmless," he drawled.

"Uh-huh. Like a cornered polecat with ten-inch claws."

"Cornered? Now, I wonder what put that notion into your pretty head? I'm free as the breeze." His voice dropped to a suggestive whisper. "And I'd never claw you. You could bet your bottom dollar on it."

"Oh, Mr. Winston," she crooned, mocking the voice of the fan as she'd done before, "the things you do say! You make a poor girl's heart go pitty-pat."

He chuckled again. "Okay. Enough. Truce?"

"Truce," she agreed cheerfully. Yet she didn't feel relaxed, and inhaled deeply on her cigarette. The truth was that everything about this evening made her nerves stretch tight. The unwanted feelings simmering inside her made her nervous. The thought of the important new singing job made her nervous. It was, after all, going to be "the big time." And the anticipation of the evening stretching ahead of her, alone with Dave Winston at his secluded country home, made her stomach flutter. She felt like a groupie, drawn to Dave, dangerously close to melting when he touched her, wanting more when he'd kissed her. . . .

"Maybe I shouldn't have come," she muttered, tapping the cigarette against the ashtray before taking another long drag.

"Hey," he growled. "Relax, Ellen, will you?" He raised one hand in a solemn oath. "This ole farm boy hereby promises not to lay one calloused finger on you . . ." He turned one of those neon grins on her. "Unless, of course, you want me to and ask me real nice."

"Fat chance, ole farm boy!"

They both laughed a little, then rode along in silence. Ellen had a sensation of whirling through the dusk as if in a dream. Was all this actually happening to her? After years of trying, was she really going to be standing on stage with this big star? There were plenty of country-western hits about dreams coming true. It was a favorite theme. At this moment, she could pen her own ballad. The audition itself seemed a distant memory now. The hot, crowded room, the lineup of women of all ages, from teenagers to over-the-hill ex-chorus girls, all waiting to sing their hearts out, hoping Dave Winston would chose them for his group. She had been near the end of that long line of hopefuls, her stomach tying itself in knots as her time to sing drew nearer.

Dave was a gold-record man several times over and had won the Best Male Vocalist of the Year award plus dozens of others. His songs were constantly at the top of the country-western charts, and the whole world loved him. He had a quiet charm, which attracted young and old. His singing style was unique, softly soothing and intimate, a combination that caused women's hearts to melt. Ellen imagined he would be another conceited egomaniac in person. Supposedly, it was hard to be humble when the world bowed at your feet. But Dave sure didn't seem like an egomaniac at all . . . he seemed, well, just like his singing style. She shook her head to clear out those foggy images.

When her agent had set up the audition with Dave, she had agreed, not really figuring she had a chance to get the job but willing to give it her best try. The competition in the audition room was monumental. Some of the women had been in the business a long time and had plenty of experience doing backup work. Whatever it was that made Dave choose her over all the talented lovelies in the room, she was grateful. More than that . . . overwhelmed.

Dave swung the red car unto a blacktop driveway. stopping in front of a high iron gate and blinking his headlights. The gates swung open, and they drove through. Dave gunned the motor, and the car shot ahead up the long private driveway, tires squealing on the blacktop. Ellen glanced back to see the gates swing shut behind them.

"They're electronically controlled," he told her. "Look around you; this is it . . . Greyhound Acres, better known to my close friends as the Hacienda. Just don't listen to what people here say about me, Ellen. They might tell you I love my hounds almost as much as my music and more than I could love any woman." He swung the car around the looping driveway, stopping in front of the rambling, red-tile-roofed house. "Not so." He flashed her a smile. "I'd rather kiss a gorgeous woman any day. Greyhounds have cold noses."

She smiled as he slid out and came around to open her door. Charming as the day was long, but what a flirt he was, she thought. Dave quickly took her arm, ushering her toward the shallow wooden porch of the white stucco house. Even knowing he was merely trying to make time with her, she reacted to him again. No doubt about it, McKay, she told herself, Dave Winston is one helluva charmer, probably the most exciting man you've ever met, and not to be trusted an inch with real feelings.

"It looks very Mexican," she said as he opened the front door and motioned her inside. "Very colorful . . . and very *un*-Nashville."

His laugh rumbled pleasantly through the spacious foyer. "The original owner had it built from plans of a Mexican hacienda he owned in southern California. The place really faces inward, so that every room opens onto the patio. Wait until you see it. I fell in love with it the minute I laid eyes on it. When I saw the 'For Sale' sign go up, I made a wild dash for the real estate office. I was first in line, luckily, and with a good enough offer. Come on. I'll show you around." He tossed his Western hat expertly onto the iron hat rack on the wall just as a middle-aged woman wearing a crisp blue housedress and apron came into the foyer.

"Aggie, darlin', this is Ellen McKay. She's going to

be taking Lynn's place. How about making her welcome with a cup of your special herb tea?"

Ellen's eyebrows flew up. Was he putting her on? What was this—*herb tea* in a world of booze, pills and, at the least, strong black coffee?

Aggie nodded. "Maybe the young lady doesn't share your enthusiasm for herb tea, David. She seems a little flustered by your suggestion."

He flashed Ellen a crooked grin. "Aggie is a second mother to me. She runs this place and me with steel hands inside her lace gloves. Believe me, I can't leave the house without an umbrella on a rainy day. Aggie would send the National Guard out after me." He spoke with such genuine affection, Ellen felt doubly mixed-up.

"I *love* herb tea," she quickly said to the housekeeper. "I was just so surprised anyone else around here did, too. I really go for peppermint and camomile."

Aggie's face brightened. "Now, *that* one is my cure for anything that could possibly ail a person. I'll put a pot on to steep right away. Where will you be, David?"

"In the studio, as soon as I show off the place to Ellen."

The woman nodded, turning to disappear into a room Ellen assumed to be the kitchen. Dave moved a few steps closer, nodding toward an archway. "Step into my living room, said the frog to the moth. Not everyone likes the style, so don't be afraid to turn up your perky nose. Most of the floors in the house are tiled with terra cotta, which Aggie keeps polished like a mirror."

Ellen walked to the archway to survey the spacious room. The beamed ceiling was low, setting off the heavy, red-cushioned oak furniture. Several pieces of woven rattan gave the room a warm, casual look. Mexican rugs and pottery added to its charm and beauty.

"I love it!" Ellen whirled around to see it all. "You have excellent taste, Dave."

"Thanks." He moved past her to reach up and touch a huge Mexican sombrero hanging on one of the beams. "I can't take credit for the decoration. My secretary, Gwen Kelly, brought in all the Mexican items. She picked up the dolls on a trip to Mexico City last summer. I put up a heck of an argument, of course. I go for real *live* dolls, but Gwen's a tiger. You'll meet her tomorrow. She's been my right arm for two years."

Ellen fingered the bright red-and-blue skirt adorning a black-haired doll. So there was a Gwen in his life. She should have known anyone as famous and as magnetic as Dave would have a special woman. Not that it really mattered to her. Her interest here was in the job... not in the boss. Well, not quite, she admitted to herself.

"We can cut across the patio to the studio," he told her, leading the way to a sliding glass door at the end of the living room. "This opens into the courtyard. You're going to love it out there, Ellen."

She knew he wasn't being boastful. He was extremely proud of his lovely home and wanted her to see it. Apparently it had been a dream of his to own a place like this, to have his dogs and Mercedes. She could understand that. She too had dreams. Dave Winston hadn't always been on top. He had had to struggle to get where he was today in the country-music world.

They crossed the red tile space, which was shaded by tall trees and brightened by tubs of flowers. At one end of the patio there was a mirrorlike pond. The entire place had the look of a restful, romantic movie set or an exotic little park.

Ellen breathed in the clean, fragrant air, exhaling slowly, savoring the freshness. "I think it's great," she said quietly, and she shivered slightly when Dave reached out to take her hand.

He smiled down at her. "Good. You're going to be spending a lot of time here, you know. It's terrific in the worst of the summer, when we practically live in the pool. That's behind the office, along with the tennis court. You do swim and play don't you?"

She sighed and after a moment of thought, said, "I do a crazy kind of dog paddle and swing a cockeyed racket...never hit anything, of course, but I sure do try.".

His laugh was hearty, and he squeezed her hand tighter. "And I sure do like you, Ellen McKay. This has been my lucky day. I don't mind telling you when I saw that room full of would-bes this morning, I had visions of being forced, out of desperation, to hire some pushy little witch. I never expected real talent and a warm heart all in one beautiful body." He stopped at the door of the tile-roofed studio and turned to face her. The sun was sinking low, but still flooded the patio near the studio with its dying rays. Dave's intensity was almost unbearable. Ellen felt herself beginning to drift on a cloud, and she quickly got a grip on herself.

His expressive eyes slid over her body from head to toe, lingering for just a moment on hips, then breasts. "Yeh. You're beautiful, Ellen."

She blinked nervously, feeling nude under his gaze, and wishing she could believe he meant what he said. Her full lower lip trembled, surprising her with all the vulnerability stored up inside, which she didn't even know existed till this minute.

With a quick shrug, Dave opened the door. "Step right inside and see what wonders await you. The studio. After we do over the songs, I'll introduce you to the bus. That will be our home away from home for a few weeks."

She stopped suddenly on the threshold, scowling as she turned to look at him. "You're going on tour?"

"We are going on tour. You're a part of the group now, remember? We leave in a few weeks; that's why we have a lot of rehearsing to do. We'll be traveling to Ohio, Pennsylvania and New York. I'm not sure what cities they set up for us . . . probably the usual, Cleveland, Philadelphia, Buffalo, Rochester . . . the Big Apple. How does that sound?"

At the moment she was speechless. Ordinarily it would sound fantastic, but the thought of living on the same bus for weeks with Dave Winston made her blood run warmer. She just couldn't do it! And yet . . . if she wanted the job—and she *did* want it, needed it, desperately—she would have to ride off into the sunset on his bus.

He looked down at her, amusement written on his face. "Not afraid of all that togetherness, are you? Believe me, when we're on the road, we're all one big happy family. You'll see. Actually, we have the bus for riding, and a truck for the instruments and sound equipment. It does tend to be crowded, but take heart, honey, we *do* spend the nights in hotels along the route. However, since there is one small room on the bus, I think you can share it with Gwen. There are some bunks . . . uppers and lowers, for the sleepyheads in the outfit."

The news that she and Gwen would share a room didn't thrill her. Right now, Gwen was a big question mark. Her thoughts on the subject didn't make a bit of sense, she knew, because she had to be fair and wait until she met Dave's obviously dedicated "secretary" before forming any opinions. A slight smile curved her full, red lips. For all she knew, Gwen Kelly might be sixty-five and as dried-up as a stale raisin.

She stepped inside the studio, immediately amazed at its intricacy. One section of the soundproof room was encased in glass; a long, complicated control panel faced the room's microphones, music stands and speakers.

"I'm really impressed! This is a professional recording studio." She shook her head in surprise. "I didn't expect anything quite this complex."

"I do a lot of recording here, so I figured I might as well do it up right. I have a terrific technician handling the controls. He makes us sound great even when we're not. It's a talent. We record everything we sing here first, before we take it to the people downtown. How does that sound?"

She moved around the room, taking everything in, pausing at the white baby-grand piano in one corner to run her fingers up and down the keys before facing Dave.

"It sounds frightening. Would you believe that in all my years in Nashville, I've never cut a demo? I could never come up with enough money, and no one exactly beat a path to my door. Carl cut several records, at Studio B usually." She stepped away, pausing at one of the wooden music stands, where she tried on the bulky, heavy earphones, pretending the weight made her head drop to her chest. She would be fine if she could be a clown, never too serious, and always remaining several feet away from Dave. There was definitely a strong flow of attraction passing between her and Dave. She drew in her breath, removing the headgear and placing it on the stand, where she ran her finger over the polished wood. She squared her shoulders, ready to face any situation. After all, she was certainly mature enough to remain in complete control of her emotions. This job meant everything to her. It was the big time. She had waited years for this break, and she wasn't going to mess it up with some silly attraction. Working with Dave, going on the road in the tour bus with the group, acting indifferent to his charms, would add up to one big challenge. And a challenge was something she had never run away from. She would just remind herself constantly, whenever Dave was a breath away and she felt like succumbing, that her career was the most important thing in her life. She had been burned by cupid once, double-crossed by the adorable cherub. Well, she would never let that little monster zap her again with his poison arrow. Of that she was certain.

Chapter Three

DAVE WALKED OVER to the piano, motioning her to join him on the bench. "I'll run through a few of the top songs we'll be doing." He handed her the sheet music. "Jump in where it says 'backup,' and don't worry about the way it sounds. We'll go over it plenty tomorrow, until it's perfect."

When she sat down and her thigh rubbed against his, she was painfully aware of his presence. She inched away from him on the bench, ignoring his laugh.

He shook his head, amused at her reaction. "There you go again, honey, scared to death of me." He let his fingers roam over the piano keys in a soothing ballad, and Ellen soon found herself relaxing, concentrating on the music. The second time through, when Dave sang the vocals, the words of burning passion touched Ellen's heart. The notes blurred on the page, and she missed her first cue. Dave shrugged it off.

"No problem," he told her, going back to repeat it. Now she came in with the right chorus, her soft alto joining with his deep baritone. They sang several verses, and time seemed to stand still for Ellen. She found herself suspended in limbo, the music taking over her very being. When the last notes drifted away, his eyes met hers, and her resolutions faded with the music. Anticipation gnawed at her stomach. She knew Dave was going to kiss her, and even though she understood that the situation was unreal and Dave could have no commitment to her, she wanted to feel his lips on hers, wanted the smoldering fire inside her to ignite. This time she knew she would respond to his kiss. She wasn't even going to try to fight it. He leaned closer, his own desire showing plainly in his eyes.

"You're quite a gal, Ellen McKay. Quite a gal." His words were a gentle whisper as he pulled her close to his body.

Ellen's lips trembled under the soft pressure of his. Their lips clung, then moved in the quiet rhythm of the most tender of love ballads they'd sung together. There was precious harmony in the gentle kissing for Ellen ... and it seemed a blissful eternity of meeting and melding. Dave's mouth slid to her cheek and nuzzled it, while Ellen, eyes closed, moved her head slowly, relishing his touch. He kissed her brow, her nose, her other cheek, and returned to her mouth. Now the pressure was greater, and their lips were slightly parted. They savored each other, hands gentle on each other's backs. His teeth caught tenderly at her lower lip and teased it to a softly swollen ripeness before abandoning it to nibble the lobe of her ear. She moaned, and her tongue curled out to feel the roughness of his bearded cheek and taste its saltiness, spiked by the merest hint of after shave. His tongue flicked around the shell of her ear and into its inner warmth, then moved to her cheekbone, her closed, fluttering lids. The softly throbbing music in Ellen's veins changed tempo. Now it rushed, tweaking and twanging like the hot rhythms for a wild clog dance. She could feel the quickening in Dave, too, and grasped his face between her hands. Breathless, they stared deeply into each other's eyes—a moment so exciting Ellen thought her heart might burst! And then with a strange groaning sound of longing, Dave's mouth fell on hers. Lips pushed firmly apart, his tongue stroked into her mouth, demanding a response before thrusting harder and faster, faster and harder...

The sudden sound of clattering dishes parted them. Aggie crossed the studio, sputtering an apology as she set her tray on the piano. "I knocked, but I guess you were too *involved* to hear me."

Dave breathed raggedly as Ellen shuddered. A half-smile curved his lips. "Aggie," he said hoarsely, but with good humor, "your timing's lousy!"

Aggie was obviously unruffled by the scene she'd just interrupted. "Don't I know it?" She chuckled. "I *heard* you two singing a while back. Sounded perfect together... good harmony. Best I've heard in a while." She shot a look at them over her shoulder, from the doorway. "I think you've found just the right addition to your group, David."

He winked at her. "I think you may be right, Aggie."

The door slammed behind the housekeeper, and Ellen felt a new, uncharacteristic wave of shyness pass over her. She hustled over to the tea tray and poured out two cups. Dave followed her, and as their hands brushed in the exchange of cup and saucer, he smiled wickedly at her.

"It's clear you've got yourself a special place in the program now, Ellen. We'll work up some duets to try out around here and put in the show while we're on tour. I'll introduce you as the special little chickadee I've taken under my big ole wing. How's that sound?"

His words were full of double meaning, and she sipped thoughtfully at the herb tea. "I don't know if I'm ready for all that, Dave."

"Fast is the way things happen in this business. And you said yourself you've been building up to this for a long time, so it isn't as if you're a greenhorn. We could start with a duet... how about that? Maybe the one we sang last. We were good together, damned good, you know."

She nodded. "I thought so, but"—she put her cup and saucer down abruptly—"Dave, why are you rushing me?"

He munched one of Aggie's chocolate-chip cookies and washed it down with tea before answering her. "Rushing you? After all this time you've been in the business? Besides, I think the fans will like you—and us together. You'll still sing backup, but you're going to do special songs, too."

"You're being impulsive."

"I'm an impulsive guy. It's all settled."

"Just like that, huh?"

"Just like that." His lips touched the tip of her upturned nose, and his hand brushed back her soft, shining hair. He pulled away. "To work, woman," he said lightly. "We have dozens of tunes to go over tonight."

The ecstasy of the past moments between them were turned into music as they harmonized on song after song.

And somehow, in some way words could never match, Ellen felt a new and different intimacy grow between them... and her wariness of Dave's intentions toward her dissolved.

They sounded good together, and they both knew it. The last notes of the final song had just died away when Aggie poked her head in the door. She wore a faded blue chenille bathrobe and bright knit slippers, and her hair was lost in a mass of fat pink curlers.

"I left cocoa on the back of the stove for you two," she announced. "I'm going to bed. It's past midnight, you know." Without waiting for a reply, she turned and vanished, closing the door quietly. Ellen's eyebrows arched in surprise when she glanced at her watch.

"She's right. Where on earth did the evening go to? Dave, I'd better get back to my car and take my bones home to bed or I won't be fit for rehearsal tomorrow." She got up from the piano bench, stretching and stifling a yawn.

He stood up, facing her and resting his hands on her shoulders. His hands slid slowly down her arms. "Better not let Mrs. Grey see you doing that!"

"What? Who?"

"My old she-dog. She'd take you for a slick Persian cat, stretching like that, and a feline's always sure to rile her." He grinned and stroked her arms. "Fact is, you *do* feel like a silky cat."

His words tolled in her ears like a cracked bell. Carl had said exactly that once.

She pulled quickly away from Dave's arms, turning her back, leaning against the piano for support. She couldn't face Dave now. Anger was surging inside her, replacing the passion of moments before—anger at Carl and at herself. He had been the most amoral man she had ever known, at first a loving husband, then drifting from woman to woman. It was easy for him to find willing partners in the music world, that was certain. Her heart had broken slowly. Ugly distrust rose again. Would Dave be any different? He was a big name in the business, a man who could have any woman he wanted, by merely crooking his finger. For her sanity's sake, should she remain aloof and not let herself give into Dave's very inviting charms? But the music...that kiss...the intimacy....

She knew he was close behind her. She could feel his warm breath on the back of her neck.

His voice was a whisper. "Hey, Ellen, honey, I'm sorry. I thought you felt as strongly as I did. Look, I didn't mean to push."

She turned toward him slowly. "Please, Dave...drive me back to town..." The husky quaver in her voice betrayed the confusion of her emotions.

His eyes were dreamy as he let his hands slide down to her waist, pulling her close against him so that her face made contact with his hard chest. She allowed herself to rest against him.

"Do you really want to go home, Ellen? You can stay here and get a good night's sleep before your first rehearsal..." His lips were brushing against her hair, teasing and taunting her. When his hands moved to her well-rounded backside, pulling her hips tight against him, she pushed away.

"Sleep, Mr. W.?"

"Sleep, Miz McKay." His eyes twinkled.

Damn! She wanted him! It would be so easy. With one little word she could have him—for tonight, at least. His own need and passion were just as evident as her own. One night, one night of ecstasy, and then...

He tilted her face up, bending to claim her mouth in

a searing kiss. The flame was burning brightly. In a few more minutes it would be raging out of control, and there would be no going back, no stopping that fire spreading through her veins.

Then he did something so unexpected it took her breath away. He pushed her out of his arms, smiled down sweetly and took her by the hand.

"Now, about staying over—there's a perfectly comfortable guest room right next to Aggie's room...you'll be as safe as you would be in your mother's arms."

A hint of a smile curved her lips as she realized he meant exactly what he said. "It *is* late. Maybe I will stay over...but..." She glanced down at her wrinkled slacks and limp blouse. "I won't be very presentable tomorrow."

"No problem. You're about the same size as Gwen. She keeps some of her clothes in the guest room. You just pick something out. Don't worry. I'll square it with her, even though I'm sure she won't mind."

He led the way toward the door. "How about that hot chocolate?" he asked her. "It might help you get to sleep."

She shook her head, brushing a stray lock of hair from her forehead. "No, thanks. I'd rather get right to bed. This has been one long day. The audition was hard on my nerves. I'm still not sure whether I'm awake or dreaming."

"Very much awake," he assured her, his eyes smiling. They entered a long enclosed walkway leading from the studio to the house. The windows looked out over the moonlit patio on one side and the spacious backyard on the other. The water in the swimming pool glistened, and Ellen paused for a moment to look at the tranquil scene. Dave's step was brisk, and she had to trot to keep pace. They went by his pine paneled office. A brass lamp on top of a giant rolltop desk cast a dim light in the room. Floor-to-ceiling bookshelves held a line-up of country-western awards. She could see an arrangement of eight by ten photos adorning the wall above the desk.

"Friends in the business," he commented matter-of-factly.

"And those must be your big sellers." She pointed to the opposite wall, where several bright gold discs seemed to light up the darker side of the room.

He nodded, laughing. "Aggie calls this my trophy room. Actually, this is where most of my business is conducted. Gwen puts in eight or ten hours a day here, answering mail, phones, setting up interviews, things like that." He seemed anxious to pass the room, and they hurried to the end of the hall. He nodded toward the door.

"This is the number-one guest room, Ellen. You should be comfortable here. Don't worry about over-sleeping in the morning. Right before breakfast is served, Aggie rings a bell that would wake Rip Van Winkle or even the dead, maybe." He looked down at Ellen, shaking his head and sighing. "Damn my promise."

"What promise?"

"The one I made to myself, little lady." His expression was blankly mysterious for a moment. "You've really had one helluva big day, huh?"

Ellen nodded, her eyes bright but weary. She faced away from him.

"And I bet you think I've come on to you pretty strong."

She gulped and gathered her courage to put one of her fears into words. "Dave, I admit I'm attracted to you, but..." She sighed. "I can't handle a...a...I mean, if you want double duty from your new singer, bed partnering as well as backup singing"—she turned to look at him, tears stinging her eyes, "then maybe you had better choose one of the others from the audition. . . ."

He reached out, gently rubbing the tears from her cheeks with his thumbs. His voice remained quiet and husky when he said, "No way, Ellen. I want you with the group. We'll just be buddies now, okay? Keep it cool and neat till you've simmered down, got all these new wrinkles tucked under your belt."

"Aww-w, Dave," she said softly. "Thanks. I do believe you're a real good man."

"In more ways than one," he drawled, a mischievous light in those velvet brown eyes. He studied her face, then bent his head to kiss her lightly on the lips. "Good night, pretty lady . . . sweet dreams." With those words, he turned and walked down the hall.

Ellen entered her room quickly, shutting the door and leaning against it a moment. The moonlight streamed in the two windows, bright enough to illuminate the room in a soft white light. The movement of the trees in the patio cast flickering shadows on the walls.

Ellen raised her hand to her lips, touching them gently, as Dave had moments before with a soft, feathery touch teasing enough to make sleeping difficult. She smiled. Dave knew very well how the kiss would affect her. He wanted her to stay awake just a little while, anyway, to stare at the ceiling and think how it would have been if she had spent the night with him. Damn!

She sighed and flipped on the light switch, letting her eyes take in the elegantly furnished room. The cherry-wood four-poster bed and dresser stood out nicely against the pink walls and beige carpet. The brightly flowered draperies matched the chaise longue and bedspread. It would be like spending the night in a swanky hotel. Dave had told her to borrow some of Gwen's things. Ellen hoped his secretary had a nightgown stashed away. She searched through the dresser drawers. The softly subtle scent of roses tickled Ellen's nose, and she uttered a "hmph." She and Gwen *would* have to like the same perfume! She took a nightgown out of the drawer and held it up in front of her, looking at her reflection in the mirror. Her head wagged from side to side.

"Definitely not you, Ellen," she muttered. "Much too frilly and daring." Only on her honeymoon and during the first year of her marriage to Carl had she worn friv- olous nighties; then, practicality, cold bones and a lack of money made the heavier, plainer types the sensible ones to wear. Now that she thought about it, those gowns had probably turned Carl off completely. He did often make cracks about Old Mother Hubbard. She surveyed herself. Dave would like this piece of blue see-through fluff, she was sure. It was probably the only kind Gwen wore. Well, it would cover her for one night, but she knew that wearing it would only make her thoughts of Dave more vivid. She slipped out of her slacks, blouse and underthings and popped the short gown over her head, turning to look at her reflection in the full-length mirror on the door. Yes indeed, Dave would definitely like to see her in this! She turned around slowly. Every inch of her body showed clearly through the thin nylon. She turned to look at the big double bed, sighing. It was very late and the day had been long, crazy, surprising— and completely fantastic! She *should* be ready for sleep, but . . .

Dave. His kisses. "Good gravy, Marie," she muttered, and shut her eyes, her hands rising to clutch her breasts. The way he'd made love to her mouth, her ears, face, eyes, was more provocative than a thousand caresses might be from a different man. He'd teased her with the promise of ultimate lovemaking as ecstatic as she could imagine, and then some. "Buddies." That was a laugh, when his thrusting tongue had been a preview of such searing passion to come between them. Her eyes flew open. She was enthralled and gasping for breath, her chest heaving under her taut fingers.

"What a lover man you're telling me you are, Mr. David Winston." She looked into the mirror as if she could see his image reflected there. She allowed her imagination to go. She was letting the fluffy gown slip to the floor. Dave's soft brown eyes would lazily travel the length of her slender body, appreciating the curve of her hips, her smooth flat stomach, and her firm, well-rounded breasts. Then he would reach out to her. . . . Shivering, she quickly turned away from the mirror, shaking her head to clear it.

"Maybe, Ellen McKay, you should take a real cold shower before climbing into that big, lonely bed."

Chapter Four

ELLEN TOSSED AND turned until the birds were beginning to greet the first light from their perches in the trees outside the window. And she dreamed in that restless predawn slumber.

Her name and a bright, glittering star hung on her dressing-room door at Grand Ole Opry. Dave was there, standing hip-deep in congratulatory flowers, giving her moral support for her debut on the famous stage. Her knees were like wet sponge. Dave's searing kisses, meant to give her strength, merely weakened her more. When her cue came to go on stage, her legs refused for a moment to move her toward the door. Dave reached out and grasped her hand in his, leading her, as one would a child, onto the brightly lit stage. The applause in the filled theater was deafening. Ellen's spirits soared. They liked her! She felt confident, knowing she looked perfect in her dazzling red outfit. She nodded to the band, waiting for them to play the intro, then she began her song. With a sudden change of mood, the angry crowd jumped to its feet, booing and hissing. Eggs, tomatoes and stones thumped around her on the stage. Dave strode from the wings, his arms upraised, and stood in front of her. The shouting ceased instantly, as the audience settled back down in their seats. Dave sang to them, blocking her from the audience. When his song ended, the cheers were deafening. He reached behind him and pulled her next to him, his arm encircling her waist, holding her so close against him she could feel his warmth.

"This is my partner," he announced. "A new star on her way to the Hall of Fame . . . Ellen McKay."

Ellen glanced up at him, her eyes flashing her gratitude. The fans cheered again as Dave bent and planted a gentle kiss on her upturned face. The band began a familiar ballad, and she and Dave sang, their voices blending perfectly, hypnotizing the overflow crowd in the theater. When the whistles and clapping finally faded away, they walked off the stage hand in hand. In the shadows behind the scenery, Dave pulled her close, kissing her properly until she gasped for breath.

"Let that be a lesson," his deep, soothing voice teased. "You're going to have to stay with me forever. . . ." She melted into his embrace, then slipped her arms up around his neck, arching her slender body to his, responding to his kisses with unleashed passion.

The sound of a bell clanging vibrated into her subconscious. She opened her eyes slowly, blinking the sleep away, not wanting to awaken from the dream. For a moment she wasn't sure where she was. The noise continued, ear shattering. Aggie's way of waking the

household for the day, she realized suddenly. What a
dreadful awakening it was, just when she had been so
close to heaven. Reluctantly she swung her legs over the
side of the bed, stretching; then, as she stood up, bending
a few times to touch her toes. The exercise didn't erase
the dream, but it did start her blood circulating full speed,
ready for the new day.

She walked to the dresser to stare at her still-sleepy-
eyed reflection in the mirror and grimaced. How could
she face a morning rehearsal looking as if she had been
dragged through a corn field? With a quick gesture, she
tried to smooth her rumpled hair. It needed washing, but
that was impossible, since she was in a strange house,
without her trusty hair dryer. Besides, Aggie's clanging
bell sent out warnings at intervals, jangling her nerves.
She would simply have to face the day, whatever it might
bring, looking dreadful. She went to the closet to search
through the rack of clothing. To compensate for her rumpled hair, she would pick out something flattering to
wear to rehearsal. She hoped Dave would be able to
square it with Gwen. The girl would probably mop the
floor with one of her fabulous Diors if he asked her to.
Ellen sighed. If she harbored a notion that Gwen was an
older woman and a lump, that idea should have vanished
when she found the nightgown. Strictly glamorous and
sexy! The owner of this clothing obviously had a perfect
figure.

Finally, she selected a pink-and-blue plaid wrap-
around skirt, which she knew would fit her even if there
was a difference in their sizes, and she found a soft pink
V-necked sweater to go with it. Gwen had excellent taste
and obviously chose her things carefully. Ellen laughed.
She chose her wardrobe carefully, too—from the thrift
store in downtown Nashville! She sighed, brushing her

cheek against the sweater's softness. Well, for today, at least, she'd feel like a queen.

She hurried to dress, comb her hair, and apply make-up; then, by trial and error, opening one door after another, she found the kitchen. The moment she poked her head inside, Dave, sipping a giant mug of black coffee, motioned to her from where he sat at the long maple harvest table.

"Hi, there. Sleep well?" he asked her, smiling as he jumped up to pull out her chair.

"Fine," she lied, easing herself into the chair as Aggie poured a mug of coffee and set it in front of her. The light-blue slacks and turtleneck sweater Dave wore did not go unnoticed. He looked exceptionally handsome for such an early-morning hour, handsome enough to start her adrenaline perking.

"Something smells good, Aggie," she said, trying to concentrate on other things.

"I fixed grits this morning . . . and eggs and toast," Aggie said, turning back to her gleaming beige stove to scrape the scrambled eggs into a bowl and dish up the grits.

Ellen sipped her coffee slowly, her stomach starting to entertain a convention of butterflies. Food was far from her mind at the moment. All she wanted was coffee to get her going and a cigarette to calm her nerves.

"I think I'll just have toast, Aggie. I'm not much of a breakfast eater."

"Nor supper either." The housekeeper smiled in her direction. "Young woman, you're already looking like a knitting needle with pin fever."

Dave laughed. "An original Aggie saying. They ought to be put into a book." He winked at Ellen. "Eat what you want, honey. Just make sure you have enough energy to face the hours of rehearsal ahead. The crew will be straggling in any time now. They're usually rushing through that door just in time for Aggie's coffee. You're going to be a little nuts for a while, meeting everyone, but if it's any comfort, I know they're going to love you, Ellen. The guys are great, and the backup crew is terrific. We get along like a big family . . . and of course, Gwen is the greatest, right, Aggie?"

At the counter, the woman buttered golden toast, nodding. "She's a sweet girl; not a mean bone in her body."

Ellen felt a knot tighten in her stomach, and she deliberately ignored Dave and Aggie's remarks. Dave cocked his head to one side, eyebrows raised as he stared at Ellen thoughtfully.

"Do you know"—his voice was quiet, sexy—"that outfit looks terrific on you."

His tone warmed her to her toes. "I just hope your secretary won't be too furious with me for borrowing her things." Ellen picked up a piece of warm buttered toast, spread on grape jelly and nibbled at it. It was very difficult, trying to eat with those velvet eyes appraising her so closely.

"I'll explain it to her." His mouth broke into a wide grin. "Relax, will you? You're among friends, honest."

"Friends? A little too soon for that, Dave." She swallowed the toast, washing it down with more of the luscious coffee. The moment she emptied the mug, Aggie refilled it. She softened her previous words, saying "I guess I'm more nervous about today . . . well, you know, so much has happened to me since I left home to go for the audition yesterday morning. I haven't come back down to earth yet."

Dave's eyes caught hers. "Yes . . . a lot *has* happened."

The sound of car doors slammed in the driveway snapped their mesmerized gaze. In seconds the door to the kitchen burst open.

The room became a madhouse with the entrance of four band members and the three other backup singers. When Dave introduced Ellen to the group, it was obvious by their greetings that they would approve of any choice Dave Winston made. But her spirits did soar when, one by one, they welcomed her aboard. Keeping them straight in her mind was difficult . . . with four exceptions. Al "Red" Martin, the first guitarist, had the most luxurious red mane of hair she had ever seen, and the proper number of freckles to go with it. Joe Leone, the steel guitarist, had a receding hairline, to put it kindly, and was called "Mt. Baldy." Tom and Janet Adams were easy to remember. They never took their eyes or their hands off each other for very long. Their love was like a neon sign lit for all the world to see.

"Wait until you hear these boys in action, in rehearsal," Dave exclaimed. "Old P.J., here, can tickle the ivories better than anyone I've ever heard"—he shook his head, grinning—"and Sid is the best drummer in the business."

"Not so," the stocky drummer told Ellen. "Somewhere there has to be someone better, but I sure keep hopin' Dave'll never find him!"

Chuck, the tall, lanky backup singer, pulled his chair next to Ellen's and leaned close. "I hear you're going to be my partner for a while. How about it—do you think we can make beautiful music?"

Ellen laughed. "I don't think Lynn would want us to make it *too* beautiful."

Chuck winked at her. "We'll get along great."

The banter around the table continued until all of them had eaten their fill of Aggie's breakfast. Then they rose and went to their cars to get their instruments before going over to the studio.

As Ellen followed Dave, she wondered what on earth she was doing here with this famous group. They had been friendly, welcoming her without any question, accepting the fact that their leader had chosen her to fill the gap left by Lynn's taking maternity leave. She pinched herself to make sure it wasn't yet another dream.

"I'm scared," she muttered, following Dave along the walkway. Briefly she wished he would take her arm, as he had last night. His touch had given her strength, and she needed to feel that strength now. But then she remembered her dream... and her nervousness turned into something much deeper. Dave had stopped. His eyes searched her face a moment; then his sensitive mouth curved in a warm, reassuring smile.

"Relax, Ellen, honey. Everyone likes you. You're going to be warbling our tunes like an old-time bird before the day is over, you'll see."

She swallowed hard. "Have I met everyone?" She was thinking about Gwen. The walkway was narrow, and they were very close, their arms touching as they walked.

"You'll meet Rocky, my manager, one of these days. He comes and goes. Gwen should be in the office soon. She's often late, oversleeps a lot, but she makes it up to me later on...."

That was probably an understatement. Ellen bit her tongue as if she'd made the catty remark aloud. "I guess the first day on any job is a bit frightening. I want to do well, Dave."

He moved his hand to find hers, squeezing it to reassure her. She paused a moment, turning to face him. "Be patient with me, please, Dave." Her eyes searched his face, pleading.

Dave needed no more from her. He pulled her hard

against him, kissing first her forehead, then her cheeks, before letting his mouth claim hers. Ellen felt her heart thumping wildly in her chest and throat as his strength flowed through her body and she responded to his kiss.

Neither of them heard a sound. It was Ellen who opened her eyes briefly and glanced over Dave's shoulder to see the lovely blond-haired woman standing there, scowling, her mouth petulant. Quickly, Ellen pushed away from Dave's embrace. When he turned to see why, he grinned sheepishly.

"Gwen!" he exclaimed. "You have me at a slight disadvantage, speechless." He stepped quickly away from Ellen, who felt deserted, betrayed.

"Sorry if I interrupted anything." The green-eyed beauty's voice was a teasing purr.

Dave cleared his throat. "Just a good-luck kiss. Gwen, meet our new backup singer, Ellen McKay. Ellen, meet my right hand, my gal Friday, who just happens to be my favorite cousin."

"Hi." It was a stupid greeting, and Ellen wanted to vanish. Gwen's eyes were staring her up and down. She waited for Dave to say something, and the moment of silence seemed an eternity.

"Hi, yourself," Gwen finally said, smiling. "I see we have the same good taste in clothes."

"I feel dreadful about this," Ellen said quickly. "Really, I do, Gwen. I intend to have your things cleaned and returned as soon as possible, if that's all right?"

Gwen glanced down at her trimly tailored green slacks and frilly white blouse. Her jacket was draped casually around her slender shoulders. "Take your time. I'm not hard up for clothes, Ellen. No problem."

Ellen was relieved, but she was quick to notice there was not a bit of emotion in Gwen's tone. Her lovely face

was a mask, her manner cool and aloof. It was obvious
that *she* did *not* approve of Dave's free ways with her
wardrobe, even for his newest addition to the Greyhounds.

The statuesque Gwen, her long hair bouncing on her
shoulders, walked with them to the studio, talking to
Dave about the many business matters she intended to
take care of during the morning. Ellen felt a complete
stranger, eavesdropping on a private conversation. She
let herself fall behind, her eyes burning into Dave's back.
She made a hasty observation. Gwen was very protective
of her boss-cousin, and probably helped him out with
women who made pests of themselves. Well, she would
soon put Gwen straight about her own intentions. She
wanted a career, she wanted a chance to work hard, and
that was all she was going to ask of Dave or allow . . . *now*.

Dave opened the door, and Gwen swept into the studio, a princess entering her domain. He waited for Ellen,
whispering in her ear as she passed him, "Don't let the
rehearsal get you down."

"I'll try to relax," she told him, knowing there was
no way in the world she could accomplish *that* this morning. Last night, singing with him alone had been different—special, relaxed. Today, others would be judging
her . . . and those others weren't uncritical fans. They
were her fellow musicians, and the people from whom
she most wanted respect and appreciation. Theirs were
the opinions that truly mattered.

Inside the studio, the band members were warming
up. Dave went straight over to pick up his guitar from
a table against the wall and start tuning it. Tom and Janet
Adams stood with Chuck Wells at one of the tall wooden
stands, their music spread out in front of them. Ellen

waited for a moment, still feeling as if she had no right
to be in this inner sanctum of successful musicians. Dave
seemed to ignore her completely, intent only to get the
rehearsal underway. It was Janet Adams who finally fluttered her hand in Ellen's direction.

"You belong with us," she said, smiling. "We're in-
clined to forget you're new. Come on, squeeze in here
next to me."

Chuck moved over, making room for her at the stand.
"Sorry, Ellen . . . just push your way in after this. We'll
wake up after a while."

Dave was finally satisfied with the sound of the instruments as they played a short warm-up number before
starting the long practice session. Ellen found herself
slowly relaxing, keeping time with her body to the country-western rhythms she loved. She felt at ease when
Dave explained, "OK, gang, let's get with it . . . how
about taking the "Lover's Farewell" number first?
There's some tricky harmony in that chorus. We're going
to work hard on it. I do mean *hard!*" He walked over
to the band, winking across the room at Ellen. "Just jump
in there with the backup. Make yourself at home. You
belong now—remember?"

She nodded. Dave was devastatingly handsome,
standing there strumming his guitar. But, she reminded
herself, she was a working girl, intent upon making a
good impression, doing a flawless job. This was the
break she'd been waiting for, and she wasn't about to
flub it first thing by making moon eyes at her boss. She
forced herself to concentrate on the sheet of music in
front of her.

Their first effort at harmony was a bit uneven. Ellen
was aware of the fact even before Dave shook his head,
scowling as he signaled for them to begin the song again.

After a few attempts, Ellen was finally able to blend her voice with the backup group. She knew immediately when the sound was right. Dave merely nodded, urging them with a motion of his hand to go on with the song. Time passed swiftly as they repeated the same song over and over, until it was near perfection. Only then did Dave let them go on to another.

The backup group had little or no involvement in the next few songs and when Aggie crept into the studio carrying a large pot of coffee, the four went quietly to the back of the room to get cups of the fragrant brew. Ellen wished she could light up a cigarette, but the sign over the door proclaimed in large red letters that smoking was strictly forbidden. She finished the last drop of coffee just as the music ended.

"Let's try that duet we did last night, Ellen," Dave called to her. She set the mug down on the table with a thud, feeling a thrill of nervous apprehension sweep through her. It was that "something is going to happen" sensation, gnawing and miserable . . . and exciting.

They sang the ballad of love and Ellen knew they sounded great. The others listened, their expressions giving away their surprise at the perfect blend of voices. When the last note faded, P.J., still seated at the piano, shook his head.

"Man, that was great! You picked yourself a real winner in the little lady, Davey boy."

Waiting at his drums, Sid nodded, clicking his teeth. "You two were *made* to sing together."

Dave's grin widened, and he seemed relieved as he slipped his arm around Ellen's waist, hugging her. "Didn't I tell you?" He seemed to be high on the music, and her spirits soared to match his. If she had harbored any doubts about fitting in with the group, they quickly faded, with the jubilation in the rehearsal room. The atmosphere around the coffeepot was one of anticipation. There was an electric excitement in the air, an eagerness to return to work, to iron out flaws and bring out the sounds they had just heard, until everything was absolutely perfect. It was a feeling Ellen had not experienced in a long, long time, a feeling of being on top of the world, of having everything suddenly go her way.

"Let's get on with it, gang," Dave shouted above their talking as he slammed out a few clanging chords on his guitar to get their attention.

Ellen was grinning. She felt she belonged now. There was nothing tangible in the group's actions, yet there was something that told her as plainly as words that she was one of them.

As the afternoon wore on, the mood changed. Fatigue beat down their emotional highs. Dave, too, changed in front of Ellen's eyes. From a laughing, joking leader who inspired them, he turned into a surly slave-driver. Her own mood changed quickly with his. Doubts returned to plague her. Could it be her fault things were beginning to go wrong with the music? No one said anything. Her stomach ached almost unbearably when she had to sing a few bars solo, over and over again, until her timing was exactly the way Dave wanted it. Tears were close to spilling over when he stopped her in the middle of a phrase.

"Damn it, your timing is off. Can't you read the music, Ellen?"

The room was deathly silent until Chuck broke the spell. "Hey, man, take it easy. That last flub was my fault. Sorry. I'll get it right next time."

The drops of perspiration on Dave's forehead trickled down his face in tiny rivulets now. He didn't look at

Ellen, or apologize as he signaled for them to begin the song again; this time it ended with his approving nod.

As the afternoon wore on, the tension in the room began to sizzle. Ellen could feel herself going limp, shaky, dreading each new song. When a bell clanged, Ellen recognized it as Aggie's mealtime signal, an indication that work should cease, and she was so relieved she could've cried. Dave put his guitar on the table, pulled a handkerchief from his back pocket and mopped his forehead. He too seemed near exhaustion.

"OK, gang...that's it for today," he told them. "Same time tomorrow." The others packed away their instruments and music in almost complete silence, until Dave's tension-erasing laugh echoed through the room. "Hey...come on...it was a *good* day. I'm proud of you all."

Ellen leaned wearily against the music stand, not trusting her shaky legs to hold her.

Dave's gaze turned to her. "Nice going, Ellen," he told her. With his words, the room came alive with laughter and wisecracks as the crew filed out, shouting their goodbyes for the day.

Dave crossed the room to stand in front of her, his eyes searching her face. "I was rough on you," he said gently. "I'm sorry. I get that way when I want everything to go right. I'm a perfectionist by nature—consider yourself flattered, honey. I only shout at those I like." His smile was weary but warm. Ellen felt her tension melt away.

"I feel stupid, not picking up that one part—I was afraid I ruined the group." She gave him a faint smile.

He put his hands on her shoulders, shaking his head. "No way..."

At that moment Gwen came into the studio from the

office, looking as lovely as she had when she began work that morning. Her makeup was unmarred, her hair flawless, her clothing unrumpled. Everything about her spelled perfection and made Ellen want to stick out her tongue, hiss, boo, waggle her fingers.

"It was a good session, Dave," she exclaimed. "I listened to some of it . . . there were a few rough spots, but you got them worked out. . . ." She looked at Ellen as she spoke. "It's difficult to break in someone new. . . ."

"No problem," Dave told her. "Ellen did a great job." He winked at Ellen, then asked, "Are you staying for supper, Gwen? Aggie always makes enough for a small army, you know, just in case . . ."

Again Gwen's eyes swept over Ellen; a very faint, almost imperceptible smile curved her full lips. "I *would* like to get to know Ellen. After all, we will be traveling together."

Was she being friendly or sly? Ellen couldn't tell from her tone or expression. She wanted to give her the benefit of the doubt—especially because she was a little guilty about her first childish reaction to Gwen's perfect appearance.

Gwen made a face, wrinkling her nose. "But I'm sorry, I have an important meeting tonight. Maybe another time. I'll see you both in the morning." She spun around, leaving the room without another word.

"See you," Dave called after her. Ellen nodded, breathless at the woman's hasty departure. Did she approve of Dave's hiring her, she wondered?

"She's awfully pretty," she said when the door had closed after Gwen.

Dave gave a short laugh. "And I'm afraid my dear little cousin knows it, always has. But I love that gal. She's a big help to me."

Ellen nodded. "I have the feeling she is *very* protective

of you, Dave. Heaven help the woman who tries to make time with you if Gwen doesn't approve of her."

His laugh was hearty. "You're a mind reader, too. In that respect, Gwen can be a pain."

These brief words told Ellen a great deal. Dave was probably no different from the roving Carl. Maybe all men *were* alike, tomcats by nature or if given too many chances. She sighed wearily. This was the time to renew her vow *not* to get involved, no matter how attractive Dave might be . . . no matter how much he turned her on. It was time to take control of her life, to concentrate on her dreams of success, and to move forward toward that goal. She had a start up the same ladder Carl had climbed, and she wouldn't muff that chance by letting her heart go haywire.

"I really should get home, Dave," she told him. "I can call a cab to take me back to the Pizza Port, where I left my car. . . ."

He shook his head, his eyes studying her face. "No way. I brought you out here, and I'll take you back . . . but not until after dinner. You're not really in that big a hurry to get home, are you?"

She dropped her head to hide her face. Ever since she was a little girl, any lie she uttered became quickly apparent in the crimson flush that flooded her face. She couldn't chance it now.

"I really should get home early. A woman can't go forever without doing her hair and rinsing out a few things . . . nothing personal, Dave."

He chuckled. "I guess I was being selfish. I like having you here. As you might have noticed, I don't have a bunch of hangers-on. I'm a loner, except when I'm working. Usually there's just Aggie and me rattling around this house."

"Gwen must be here sometimes," Ellen reminded him,

smiling. "Her clothes certainly aren't in the closet for decoration."

Again he laughed, his dark eyes twinkling. "You're right. Gwen does stay here as often as she can. She's teaching a class in aerobic dancing at night school until July. After that, she will probably be staying here more often. She practically lives in the pool during the real hot weather."

Ellen wasn't at all surprised by this bit of information. She could visualize the lovely blonde sunning herself poolside, her slender, string-bikini-clad body tanning to perfection. She wanted to growl at the picture flashing through her mind. If there was one thing she hated with a passion, it was perfect women. She smiled. In better days, Carl had told her she gave birth to green-eyed monsters and never let them out of her sight. She had hated being jealous. It wasn't a very becoming trait, and she had fought it with every ounce of her strength. But she also had discovered her worries were not born from a flaw in *her* character or out of her imagination. They were all too real.

"Hey, you look like you're a million miles away," Dave's soothing voice spoke in her ear. "Come on, let's get to the dining room before Aggie closes the restaurant!" He was about to take her arm, but Ellen moved quickly toward the door. Dave hurried to catch up to her.

"Right after supper, I really do have to leave," she told him, injecting just a touch of brusqueness into her tone.

He raised his hand, palm out. "Peace, squaw. I don't want to go on the warpath."

She didn't smile, but hurried through the walkway to the house, not talking. Just as they reached the kitchen door, Dave took her arm, holding her back.

"OK, Ellen, what's wrong? All of a sudden there's a heavy wind blowin' in from the cold north. Care to talk about it?"

She bit her lip as she shook her head. "There isn't anything to talk about," she told him finally.

He was standing very close, a breath away, looking down at her with that disconcerting gaze. Ellen reached out to open the kitchen door. "I'm just tired, Dave. This has been a long, hard day for me. My nerves are strung out as tight as rubber bands."

His gentle tone warmed her. "I'm sorry, honey. Blame the nerves on me. I shouldn't have jumped on you when you were trying so hard. I'm not perfect. I guess it's time you found that out. I have a rotten temper, one you're going to see in action plenty while we're on tour. But, I cool down as fast as I boil up, so just hang in there, OK?" He was scowling slightly. Could he be begging for *her* understanding?

She nodded, and he seemed relieved and happy as they passed the kitchen. Aggie's cooking sent heavenly odors drifting through the air to tickle their nostrils.

"Oh, goodness," Ellen exclaimed, laughing. "I just discovered I'm starving."

Chapter Five

THE HARVEST TABLE in the dining room was set with English bone china, crystal goblets and shining sterling silver. Dave played the gallant host, seating Ellen and making a mock bow before taking his own place at the head of the table. When Aggie brought in steaming bowls of vegetable soup, Dave nodded toward the third place setting.

"Expecting company, Aggie?"

She nodded. "I thought Gwen said she'd decided to join you after all. But she went to the den to make a phone call—"

"And here I am, you lucky people." Gwen's musical voice came from the doorway as she swept elegantly into the room—still flawless, Ellen was quick to note. "I made a quick phone call and cancelled my plans until tomorrow. I do want to get better acquainted with our new member." She flashed Ellen a pearly-toothed cover-girl smile. "I hope you two didn't want to be alone. I mean . . . I'm not interrupting anything, am I?"

Dave stood up and pulled her chair out for her. "Of course not, angel. We're glad you decided to join us. I'd really like you two to be good friends." He flashed a smile first to Gwen, then Ellen.

"It can't be very easy starting in a new group," Gwen said, dipping into the bowl of soup Aggie had just placed before her. She glanced across the table at Ellen. "I know what a tyrant Dave can be at times. He's a growly bear . . . but he can be like Gentle Ben too." Her words were a purr, made softer by her southern drawl.

If Gwen meant to confuse her, it was working. Ellen found herself unable to enjoy the soup. She had seen both sides of her new boss. Could she stand the pace he demanded?

Dave scowled for a moment. Then he grinned at Ellen, his enthusiasm giving him a boyish look. "Do you think you might be ready to cut the ice on the Opry stage Saturday night a few weeks from now? I'm booked for a one-night special appearance on the late show. One of those 'surpise' celebrity deals they spring on the fans now and then."

Ellen was quick to notice the frown flicker across Gwen's face before she said, "Isn't that taking a big chance, Dave? Why don't you try out the new grouping on tour first? I mean . . ." She shrugged her slender shoulders. "Ellen has never sung at the Opry, has she?"

"Gwen is right—I'd be a complete wreck, Dave. Do you really think I can do it?"

"If I wasn't sure you'd be able to do it, I wouldn't have brought it up. I think we should polish up the duet and give it a try. If the audience at the Opry likes us, we're home free." He winked at her. "I think they're going to love you, Ellen McKay."

She heard Gwen sigh, but the young woman's face showed no emotion. "What about an outfit, Dave? Will Ellen wear jeans and a red-checked shirt and a black hat, the same as the rest of the backup group?"

"I hadn't thought about that. It's a good thing I have you around to take care of the details, angel." His dark eyes appraised Ellen thoughtfully, while Aggie removed the soup bowls and set plates of crisp southern-fried chicken, hush puppies and cucumber salad in front of them.

"No. With her figure, I visualize Ellen wearing bright-red, tight-fitting pants, spangled shirt, white vest, boots and hat." He looked from one to the other for a reaction. "How does that grab you both? Come on! Be honest."

Ellen couldn't hold back her laughter. "Are you a mind reader too, Dave? Ever since I was knee high, I've had a picture of myself singing on the stage of Grand Ole Opry in a bright red outfit—one the audience can't miss."

His hearty laugh joined hers, sending a tingle up her spine. "Then that's settled. Red it will be." He glanced at Gwen. "How about it, cousin? Can you arrange something with Max?"

Gwen nodded, although Ellen didn't think she appeared exactly pleased. "Of course. But really, you two—bright red? She doesn't seem the type. I see her in an old-fashioned, high-necked dress, you know"—she gestured with her well-manicured hands—"the kind with ruffles."

Ellen felt her enthusiasm waver as Gwen's doubts crept over her. Maybe she was right. A red outfit might

be like wearing flashing neon lights. Dave quickly came
to the rescue, shaking his head.

"Can it, Gwen. It's going to be red. That's it. One
thing's for certain, people will sure as heck sit up and
take notice. A gorgeous gal all spangled and bright, with
a terrific voice—and what do you have?"

Gwen shrugged her thin shoulders, her mouth drawn
in a pout. *"I* don't have anything, Davie, dear. This is
your baby; you dress it."

Now she was reduced to an "it." Ellen fumed in-
wardly. But Gwen was probably right. Who was she
kidding? No one in Nashville knew Ellen McKay unless
they frequented the little two-bit honky-tonks where
she'd barely made a living from her singing. For those
gigs, she wore blue jeans, a denim shirt and a straw hat,
because she couldn't afford a classy outfit and the customers wouldn't have known the difference if she'd appeared on stage in a diamond-studded jump suit.

Dave's dark eyes flashed sparks. "What you have—
to answer my own question—is a big hit." His voice
was so low and firm and fierce that it made Ellen gasp.

Gwen offered a smile and raised her hand in peace.
"Ooops! I guess I did it again, didn't I, David? Sorry.
You know I can't resist a crack now and then. I'll put
a bridle on my tongue for the whole rest of the evening,
all right?"

"All right." With Dave's growled reply, the subject
was closed and they were able to appreciate Aggie's
delicious meal. Ellen felt marvelous. She'd never, ever
had a champion before; she'd never, ever even dreamed
of having one. The talk remained quite safely on neutral
topics after that, until Gwen finally pushed her chair
back.

"I think I'll go for a walk and work off some of these

calories. Bye, bye, you two." She blew them each a kiss.

They watched her disappear into the hallway and heard the front door close. Dave leaned back, sipping his cup of herb tea while Ellen stirred magnolia-blossom honey into hers.

"You'll get used to Gwen," he told her. "Sometimes, because she's family, she forgets herself and tries to take over. Rocky, my manager, has had quite a few run-ins with her, so nowdays she usually behaves when he's around. She's OK when you understand her."

Ellen nodded, wondering about her own ambivalent feelings. Being here with Dave, in his magnificent dining room, was like acting a starring role in a play. The mahogany furniture, bone china and crystal were luxuries she wasn't used to. She and Carl had eaten their meals at the kitchen counter in their cheap little two-room apartment. When success finally brought him big money, they broke up. She had stayed in the drab apartment, struggling to keep up the monthly payments. Her thoughts spun in her head as she looked around the room at the obviously expensive original wall hangings, the glistening cut glass, the well-stocked bar. What would it be like to be married to a man as successful as Dave Winston? She smiled at the idea, letting her thoughts wander. If she wanted a new outfit, she could go out and buy the very best—and not worry about pinching pennies for six months to pay for it. If she felt like having thick, juicy steak for supper, she'd tell Aggie and it would be taken care of. But the comfort wouldn't be what made it all sheer heaven. Dave would be. Even a plain life with him...

"I think I've lost you." He broke into her thoughts. "You've been somewhere miles away."

She laughed, starting guiltily. "Uh, would you believe

my dreaming of just standing on stage at the Grand Ole Opry—and being scared half to death?"

"Not for a minute! But if that's what you're selling, I'll buy . . . for now."

The tone of teasing threat made her smile, but the warmth of his eyes made a warning light flash in her brain. "Dave, I really do have to leave . . ."

He shrugged. "Okay, Ellen. But, first I have to phone Rocky and talk over the tour. That should take about thirty minutes. You make yourself at home, and I'll meet you by the car—the blue Ferrari." He held up his hand. "I'll drive you back to town then. I promise."

When he had headed back to his office, Ellen decided to go for a short walk around the grounds. The air was pleasantly warm, with a hint of the long, hot summer to come, and the estate was alive with many varieties of colorful singing birds. She stood staring around her for a moment before walking to the tennis courts, where she shook her head in disbelief.

"It's like a country club. . . ." she exclaimed, then quickly looked around to make certain no one was within hearing.

Somewhere ahead she could hear dogs barking. David's greyhounds, she reasoned, quickening her pace, eager for a glimpse of the animals he loved second to his music. She wanted to know everything about Dave, what he liked and disliked. There was no denying that she was more than attracted to him. She had never been one to indulge in fantasies, but in the brief time since meeting Dave Winston, she'd had more than her share. And she had only known him two days! Those two days seemed a lifetime.

She paused, watching a butterfly take off from a weed stalk, do a few loop-de-loops and depart for another stalk.

She sighed. Her experience with Carl should have taught her to beware of men in the business. Dave was world-famous. He had all sorts of gorgeous, desirable women interested in him. And he probably made love to many of those women. If she wanted a chance at real love and a lifetime of happiness, she had better look elsewhere, and not let herself be taken in by Dave's tantalizing charms. One musician had been enough. Lord, her emotions and thoughts were doing loop-de-loops wilder than that butterfly!

She heard laughter as she rounded a bend in the path. Ahead, she could see the kennel and fenced-in runs. Someone was already there—the caretaker perhaps. She hurried toward the building, stopping in the open doorway. There, brushing a sleek greyhound . . . heads almost touching, were Dave and Gwen. They hadn't seen her, and she turned quickly to retrace her steps.

The greyhound's ears perked up when he saw her, and a rumbling growl in his throat grew into a bark. Both Dave and Gwen looked up as Ellen moved away.

"Ellen," Dave called, ". . . wait. I'm glad you came down here. Rocky was out, so I thought I'd visit my pals here for a minute before driving you back. I wasn't sure you'd be interested, but now that you're here, I'd like to introduce you to Fleetfoot and Gray Arrow, my prize racers. . . ."

There was nothing to do but go into the kennel and, once there, to exclaim honestly over his sleek animals. "They're beautiful," she said, watching Gwen run a brush over the dog's slender body.

Dave petted the animal's head. "Fleetfoot has won every race I've entered him in. Not bad for a teen-ager, wouldn't you say?"

Ellen nodded. She didn't know much about dog racing

and she wasn't too sure she wanted to learn about the sport, despite her fascination with Dave's interests. She found horse races exciting. But watching a bunch of undernourished-looking dogs run around a track was something else. She shook her head, her hair bouncing on her shoulders as she did so.

Dave motioned her to follow him into the kennel. "Come on, I'll show you around." Gwen stopped brushing and smiled sweetly.

"These dogs are Dave's special loves. Not many women stand as good a chance at getting his real affection."

Ellen walked past her, ignoring the remark, which was obviously meant to discourage. "One quick look, Dave, and then I really do have to get back to the city to pick up my car, before the police tow it away." She caught up with him, and they walked to the end of the building, past a room of blue ribbons and trophies, another filled with boxes of dog food, vitamins, leashes, harnesses, ointments, anything a dog might need. There was a small indoor exercise track at the end of the building, and finally, a large fenced area with a door opening to an outside run. There, in a corner, another sleek greyhound rested in apparently perfect contentment.

Dave waved toward the dog. "This is Gray Arrow. He's won his share of trophies for me. Most of those blue ribbons you saw were his. He can catch up to that speedy rabbit every time."

Ellen cringed, a horrible vision crossing her mind. "The dogs chase poor little rabbits? Oh, I think that's horrid, Dave! What happens if they catch them?"

Dave laughed. "Do you really want to know? They munch and crunch a lot, of course."

Ellen turned to leave, shuddering, feeling utterly repulsed. "I've seen and heard quite enough...."

He reached out to take her arm and restrain her. His touch made her tingle. "Wait a minute, Ellen," he said. "I was kidding. Obviously you've never been to a dog race. The rabbit is phoney. It moves around the outside of the track, high enough for the dogs to see it. They think it's the real McCoy and run like crazy to catch it. Simple?" He raised his right hand. "Not one bit of munching and crunching... honest."

Ellen walked toward a screened stall where a female greyhound was nursing four tiny pups. Dave came up beside her. "Cute, aren't they?" He spoke quietly. "That's Lady Fleetfoot with her first litter. If they run half as fast as their dad, I'll be happy."

Ellen watched one of the pups stumble away from its mother, its tiny legs giving way now and then, sending it collapsing like an awkward colt. She laughed at the dogs' antics. "They sure are cute, Dave," she said, turning to look up at him, then wishing she hadn't. He was so close, the scent of his after shave tickled her nose. Musk, she noted, the scent guaranteed to attract women. Well, not this one. This woman fully intended to pretend she was immune, anyway. "I think I'd like to go now," she told Dave.

He nodded. "Sure thing, but first, I just found out about a party at Lenny Burton's, Friday after next. I'd like you to go with me so I can introduce you to the Nashville bigwigs. If you don't have a fancy evening gown hanging in your closet, get one. I'll give you an advance on your salary if you need it. I want you to knock 'em all dead. If you want Gwen to help choose something, ask her. That gal can pick clothes... and spend money with the best of 'em."

Ellen's forehead creased in a frown. "I've never been

to big party here in Music City, believe it or not. Carl and I didn't socialize much in the early days of our marriage...." She drew in her breath in a long sigh. Would she be able to handle it? She squared her shoulders. "It sounds great. Who will be there?"

"Everyone. Tammy, Roy..." He gave her a soul-warming smile. "You'll love every minute."

Ellen's eyes widened. "If you mean Tammy Wynette and Roy Clark...I'll faint." As soon as she said it, Dave reached out and took her firmly by the shoulders, shaking her so hard that her hair fell onto her face. She pulled away, pushing the wisps back in place. "What was that for?"

"You're so damn insecure that it burns me up. Look, you've got a voice, Ellen, a talent that's going to get you places—right to the top if you'll let it. But you're going to have to help the cause along, you know. You can't just sit back and wait for it to happen. These big bashes are fun once in a while. Lenny lives on Old Hickory Lake, in a mansion big enough to house an army, with a swimming pool large enough for the Olympic swim meets—"

"I'll sure try to handle it, because I'm determined to succeed in this town."

"Good girl. We'll talk about it more tomorrow, but remember, I'll be picking you up in my Mercedes. Sorry, I don't own a white Caddy." He winked at her, and their eyes met for a moment and held, until, with an effort, Ellen looked away.

"I'll buy the slinkiest gown in town, if I can have a long lunch hour to start looking. After all, the Friday after next isn't that far away."

"It's a deal. I want you to look your best. This is an important hoedown, angel. The guest list includes a couple of big New York producers, a TV executive looking for talent for a special TV series, reporters from Associated Press and several magazines . . . you name it. As I said, everyone will be there. So polish up your brass bells and wear them, OK?"

Determination swept over Ellen like a wave rushing toward the shore on a windy day, gaining strength as it went. If she had a chance to sing at that party, to show what she could do, maybe one of those VIPs would sign her up. It had happened to others—why not to her? At any rate, it was worth dreaming about for one night. Not that she wasn't grateful to Dave for hiring her . . . but she knew very well that this job lasted only till Lynn returned. Besides, it wasn't safe to live too close to an explosives factory. She had the feeling that the closeness she and Dave would be forced to share day after day, in rehearsals and on stage, would become charged, and could explode at any time.

"I think I want to leave *now.*" This time she started back toward the path. Dave's footsteps crunched on the gravel behind her, and she walked faster.

Ellen leaned her head back against the soft fur upholstery in Dave's low-slung shiny blue Ferrari and listened to the country-western music pouring from the stereo radio. Her auburn hair was fluffed around her shoulders as they sped along the highway toward town. Dave looked over at her a long moment, and she turned to face him.

"You better keep your eyes on the road, or your nice little car will end up a pile of twisted metal . . . and us with it."

He chuckled. "Sorry, but you make quite a picture, Ellen McKay. You're beautiful, you know. It's against my better judgment to take you back to that parking lot for your car. I'd much rather drive you to your door and come in for a beer."

"Is that any way for one buddy to talk to another?" she asked in a teasing tone. Then, to change the subject, she asked, "How many cars do you have, anyway? A Mercedes, a Ferrari—what else is hidden away in your garage?"

He laughed. "Just the two—honest. I'm not a car snob. But now that I finally have a few bucks rattling around in my jeans, I might as well use 'em to buy the things I like, right?"

"What, no Porsche?" she said teasingly.

"Maybe next. Who knows? What kind would you like? Your wheels have seen better days, that's for sure."

"Maybe that Porsche someday. It's on my dream list. And I intend to make that list come true."

She tapped her finger on the purse in her lap, then opened it and took out her cigarette case. "Darn . . . I'm out of smokes."

"Halleluja! I'd be glad if I never saw you with another one again."

"I don't smoke up a storm, like some people," she said defensively, "I just have one once in a while to keep my hands out of trouble."

Dave turned to grin at her. "I'll be downright pleased to take on the job of keeping your hands busy, ma'am. Can't guarantee 'out of trouble,' though."

She wrinkled her nose at him. "Just keep your mind on driving, Mr. Winston. I am not interested in romance. . . ."

"That's a damned lie, Ellen. You just have some stupid notion you can't trust a man again. Well, let me tell you, I intend to change that idea before too long. I'm *not* Carl . . . remember that."

He pulled into the parking lot, where it seemed to Ellen it had been a year and a day ago she'd left her Malibu. At first sight of the car she smiled, but then moaned. "Oh, no . . . the front tire is flatter than my kitchen table. I don't own a spare. That was on my 'want' list too!"

They got out of his car and went over to examine the damage. "Well, I'd say anyone who drives a car this old, on tires this smooth, deserves to be stranded." He stood shaking his head, mischief in his dark eyes. "Looks like you're going to have to give me that beer I mentioned a while back, then we'll take care of getting your wheels rolling again."

The smile he flashed her was designed to melt a woman's heart. In spite of her very good intentions to keep some distance between herself and Dave, she nodded, *not* because of the smile, she assured herself. She had no other choice at the moment. Buses were slow at night, and she couldn't afford the taxi fare across town, that was certain.

"Best I can come up with is a glass of wine, cheap wine. And that'll be your only reward for doing a good deed."

"We'll see." He ushered her back to the Ferrari, closed the door after her and went around to slide in behind the wheel. He leaned over to lightly brush her cheek with his lips, just enough to start that tingle inside her again.

"Darn!" she exclaimed, nervously tapping her fingers on her purse. "I wish I had a cigarette!"

When she snapped on the light to her apartment a short time later, the place seemed smaller and more dismal than it had when she had left it the previous day. Her overnight stay in Dave's magnificent mansion had accomplished that.

"Sorry about the place," she muttered, picking up a newspaper from the worn couch, folding it and depositing it in the wastebacket under her discount-store desk. "Make yourself at home, and I'll see what I can come up with in the way of wine." She saw his eyes take in the cramped space and she was glad she couldn't read his mind. He sat down on the couch while she went to the refrigerator to pull out a half-empty bottle of white wine. "There isn't much choice in this bar," she told him, pouring two glasses. "Sorry."

Dave reached for the phone. "Let me make a call to a friend of mine who runs a garage in town. He'll fix that tire for you and tow your car over here." The matter was taken care of in seconds. "No problem. Your buggy will be waiting in the morning."

He took the glass she still held for him, raising it in a toast. "Contrary to what you might think, honey, I do not drink imported champagne with every meal. Here's to you and your new career...."

"I'll certainly drink to that!" She sipped the wine and then smiled broadly. She gave him a wistful smile. "I wish I had your confidence in me. I'm *ready* for fame and fortune...I want them both more than anything. I've been broke and struggling in honky-tonks long enough. That's why I'm so grateful to you for this chance, Dave, and why I don't want to let anything get in the way of making it."

He stood up. "I wouldn't have hired you if I didn't think you'd be an asset to the group, Ellen." He moved rapidly to the door. "Gotta run. I want to work on a song tonight, one I hope to have in shape for that new album." He winked at her, but there wasn't his usual devilry in it. "Thanks for the wine," he said softly, and then eased out of the door almost before Ellen could realize he was going.

She put the chain latch on and rested her back against the door. What on earth had sent Dave skittering home that way?

Chapter Six

ELLEN DIDN'T REALLY hear the alarm at first. She only responded to the jangling, insistent sound. It seemed to grow louder, and she fumbled to find the clock on her nightstand to get rid of the annoyance. The ringing continued, and she pulled herself up in bed, groaning.

"The telephone...at this hour?" She reached for it, yawning, trying to come back to the real world. Maybe it was Dave. Could he have changed his mind about her? He'd left so abruptly.

Adrenaline shot through her, and she grabbed the receiver. "Hello...This is Ellen McKay."

A man's voice rumbled in her ear, and for a brief moment she was sure it was Dave disguising his voice to tease her or make sure she would be on time for rehearsal. The voice sounded very familiar.

"Who is this?" she asked, scowling into the phone. She had an unlisted number, one she had given out to Dave, a few of her friends, her agent. . . . She bit her lip hard, remembering one other person who had her number. "Carl?" she almost shouted into the phone. "What on earth do you want? It's only seven o'clock here, you know." She sure was wide awake now, and really puzzled by his call. It had been months since she had heard from him, and then he had only called to gloat about his great success.

"You're coming to Nashville?" she gasped, shaking her head. "I'm busy, Carl. I have rehearsals. I won't have time to see you. Anyway, I think it's best if we stay miles away from each other. We have nothing to say, really."

He persisted, and so did she. The last person she wanted to have slither back into her life was Carl Kern. She hung up the phone while he was still talking, and some of her old bitterness returned. She had been afraid Carl might play the role of the "bad penny," but hearing his voice had been a shock nonetheless.

"You had better not show up at my door," she muttered, pulling on her robe and stomping angrily to the kitchen to make her morning coffee. The magic of the previous forty-eight hours vanished as memories of the years with Carl flashed through her mind. She slammed an empty coffee mug on the counter. "Damn you, Carl!" Tears stung her eyes. "I will *not* let you push your way back into my life!"

Ellen glanced at her watch, moaned at the lateness of the hour and tossed down the last of her second cup of coffee. She would have to hurry to make rehearsal on time, and she certainly didn't want to be late! She was sure Dave would have her head.

When she went to the door, she scooped up the morning paper, pausing briefly to glance inside at the city-entertainment news. Bold print glared at her. "Dave Winston hires new singer." One of her own publicity pictures, small but clear, smiled at her from above the article. She shook her head. The news item was a total surprise to her. Dave's publicity man and her agent had done their work well . . . and *very* quickly. On another morning, the piece in the paper might have thrilled her. Now she could only wonder how far the news had reached. Had it been picked up by the Associated Press, so that Carl might have seen it? Was that why he had phoned? She tossed the paper onto the table near the door and hurried out, shaking her head. That wasn't likely. She hadn't been with Dave that long. No one out in California could possibly know she had been hired by him just a couple of days earlier.

True to his word, Dave's friend had fixed her tire and brought her car to the lot next to her apartment. She thought about the article on the drive across the city to the suburbs and Greyhound Acres. Her ego had been given a slight boost when she read the item, she had to admit. Her career to date had not generated anything more than "appearing tonight" on a sign near the door of a sleazy nightclub.

Carl's phone call still puzzled her, taking the edge off the good feelings she had about the newspaper item. He had never contacted her for any *good* reason, so she couldn't expect it now. She wanted to put Carl, and her years as his wife, out of her mind now, to think of that time simply as short chapters in what she hoped would be the thick book of singer Ellen McKay's life.

Greyhound Acres appeared ahead, and Ellen felt a

rush of happy excitement. The other members of the group were assembled in the studio, tuning their instruments, warming up with snatches of songs, killing time until she arrived. Dave was pacing the floor near the piano, going over the sheets of music he held in his hands, when she entered. He looked up, his facial muscles tight.

"You're late," he snapped. "Rehearsals start at eight o'clock *sharp*."

"I'm sorry. I ran into traffic." Lame excuse, she knew, and felt her face burn as she took her place at the music stand with Tom and Janet Adams and Chuck Wells. It was obvious they had been waiting for her. It was obvious too that Dave was doing his best to restrain himself. She had the feeling that if she did anything wrong during the rehearsal, anything at all, she would feel—and hear— Dave's annoyance burst into anger.

The morning passed quickly, with the group's going over and over several of the songs they would sing in upcoming performances. Ellen kept her mind on her work. Dave was a perfectionist, and here, at the studio, he was a slave driver, demanding the best, and getting it, from his musicians. Once, her eyes aching with fatigue, Ellen misread her music, coming in seconds too soon with the first notes of the background humming. In those seconds, Dave spun and slapped his music on the piano, sending the sheets of paper across the polished surface.

"Damn it, Ellen, can't you pay attention to the music? Maybe what you need is more sleep."

"I'm sorry," she muttered, wishing she could strike back but not wanting to anger him more. She needed this job. It was vital to her future, and she would bow and scrape if she had to to keep it, but her small mistake didn't justify his yelling. "I'll be more careful," she murmured.

He nodded, giving the signal to begin again. The hours ticked by, and as before, the rehearsal ended with a duet between herself and Dave. She knew they sounded great together. Their voices were that rare phenomenon of perfect blending.

"We're going to cut a record, Ellen," Dave said when the last notes of the romantic ballad faded into silence. "You and me. Real soon." No one in the rehearsal room moved a muscle. It was as if everyone knew that something very special had just been announced.

Ellen, standing next to Dave, looked up at him, shaking her head in disbelief.

A voice in the doorway boomed out. "I'll say you're going to. And day-before-yesterday isn't too soon."

Ellen followed Dave's glance toward the door, where a tall man with the build of a football linebacker stood puffing on a cigar.

Dave motioned him into the room. "Hey, Rocky... how long have you been eavesdropping on the rehearsal?"

"Long enough to see and hear just what you mean about this little lady." He strode over to Ellen, extending his big, pawlike hand. "I'm Rocky Lane...the manager of this ragtag outfit." He stepped back to let his narrow steel-gray eyes sweep over her. He walked around her, still appraising. Finally he stood in front of her and grinned. He turned to Dave, who looked smug. "For the first time since I've known you, you've managed to do something right, hiring this little bird. I'm going to set something up fast. I'd say you two could hit the charts overnight when we get a record out there on the market. Leave it to me, Dave."

"Don't I always?" Dave moved closer to Ellen, letting his arm encircle her waist. It was a casual move, but one that filled her with as bright a glow as the praise of her singing and the promise of an album. "What do you think now, Ellen?" Dave's enthusiastic whisper feathered her ear.

Ellen couldn't suppress a happy smile. "I think it sounds like a wonderful dream! I just hope you know what you're doing."

"Hey!" Rocky said. "I'm the best in the business. I can spot a sure thing a mile off." He spoke with the confidence of a winner, the unlit cigar still between his teeth. "I'll get on it right away." He turned, waving to the others, and was gone as quickly as he had come.

At noon, Aggie brought in a heaping tray of sandwiches and a pot of coffee. The tension in the rehearsal room was momentarily put aside. The break was needed, and everyone talked at once, anxious to unwind before the afternoon session. Lunch was almost over when Gwen entered the studio, carrying a stack of boxes. She brought them over to Ellen, who had finished her sandwich and was talking to Janet Adams about their country-western backgrounds.

"I picked up your outfit for the Opry show," Gwen said, putting down the boxes." I think these things are going to fit perfectly, Ellen. You and I seem to be about the same size." She winked as she spoke.

Ellen put down her coffee and ran over to tear open the boxes. The bright red satin jeans and spangled shirt and white vest, hat and boots looked very expensive. Ellen knew from the name on the boxes that they came from the best place in town—Max's—the place where all the stars bought their sensational outfits. Her eyes widened as she felt the material and ran her fingers over the rhinestones on the vest.

"They're great!" she exclaimed, glancing over at the piano, where Dave was standing. His gaze was directed her way. She held up the bright shirt, and he gave her the A-OK sign.

Ellen smiled at Gwen. "Thanks for picking these out for me. I certainly appreciate it." She folded the outfit and packed the items neatly back in their boxes. "I can't wait to wear them!"

Gwen laughed. "No problem. You're one of us now, Ellen. We help each other out whenever we can, right, Janet?"

"That's right. It's a terrific crew to work with," Janet agreed. "All for one and one for all."

Gwen's smile seemed genuine, and her tone oozed warmth. Had Dave spoken to his cousin, or had she decided Ellen was not a schemer after all? For whatever reason, the secretary's attitude had mellowed. Ellen was pleased. "Maybe you could go shopping with me later, Gwen. I want to start right away to find just the dress for that big party. It sounds real important, from what Dave tells me."

Gwen nodded. "One of the biggies, I'd say. If you want to impress anyone at all in the business, that's the place to do it."

Dave came up beside them. "Not giving away any of my secrets, are you, cuz?"

Gwen shook her head. "Just advice, Dave, dear. Your indiscretions are completely safe. My lips are sealed."

He held a fist in front of her nose, playfully threatening. "You didn't tell my favorite singer we're going to do our duet at that gathering of the country-music greats, did you? I deliberately kept that bit of news from her until her feet thawed out." His smile was downright wicked, and Ellen felt her heart pound.

Janet's thin eyebrows arched. "Why, Dave, how do

you know she has cold feet?" she teased.

His smile widened, and he reached out to put his arm around Ellen's waist. "I found that out last night. Tell them, honey."

Ellen pulled away, her face burning with color, the sight of which sent the two other women into a fit of giggles. At that moment she could have strangled her famous boss quite cheerfully.

The rehearsal went on far into the afternoon before Dave finally called a halt. Ellen drove her own car into town with Gwen following, to one of the most exclusive dress shops in the city. With the help of Gwen and her impeccable taste in clothes, Ellen quickly decided on a lavender voile cocktail-length dress with spaghetti straps, form-fitting bodice and free-flowing skirt. The moment she saw herself in it in the dressing-room mirror, she knew it was just the one she wanted. Gwen gave hasty approval as she stood back to admire Ellen's choice.

"You're going to bowl over everybody there, Ellen!" Gwen rolled her eyes. "Wait until David casts those big browns of his on you in this dress. He's already crazy for you, hon. This dress should knock him out."

Ellen smiled. "We do seem to have hit it off from the moment we met. Your cousin is a terrific guy, Gwen."

The blond hair bounced on Gwen's shoulders as she nodded. "I guess I'm a . . . well, let's face it—I'm a mother hen around him. You can't pretend you didn't notice that. But, honestly . . . if you knew how many little groupies and ambitious hussies go after him. Ellen, some gals will do just about anything—try to pick him up for a date or maneuver him to a hotel room." She sighed, shaking her head. "Sometimes I don't see how he can stand it. So I try to run interference when I can. I must admit, when I first saw you, I thought you might be out to get what you could from Dave, but he set me straight, pronto. I understand you were married to Carl Kern." Her eyebrows arched. "He's not bad. I've seen him on TV a couple of times. And met him once when he came to Greyhound Acres to see Dave."

That casually delivered piece of news made Ellen's breath catch in her throat. Dave had given no hint that he knew Carl, and there was no reason she knew of for him to keep that bit of information a secret. She pretended to study her flattering gown in the mirror, letting her fingers caress the soft material, but her mind went back to her early-morning phone call from Carl.

"I guess Carl wanted to join Dave's group a few months ago," Gwen said. "But Dave wasn't interested." She shrugged. "He said something about Carl's not being too dependable."

"That's for sure," Ellen agreed. "Look, Gwen...I'd rather not talk about my ex-husband if you don't mind. I want to keep him out of my life and thoughts. Dave has given me this terrific chance, and I want to concentrate all of my energy on making good. I sure don't want to let Dave down. Don't want to let myself down either."

Gwen brushed her long hair back over her shoulder in a casual gesture. "Sure. I don't blame you a bit. If I know my dear cousin, he's going to push you right to the top of the charts...overnight. You had better be ready for fame and fortune, Ellen, and so quick it can leave you breathless." Her smile was as bright and toothy as that of any model for a magazine cover. "That dress should give your career a big boost."

Ellen laughed. "Then I'll take it! I need all the help I can get. I'll let you in on a secret, Gwen. I intend to make Female Vocalist of the Year! Some year. But oh, hon, right now I feel like I'm just dreaming...or plain crazy. My whole life's turned upside-down in less than a week. I'm dizzy!"

"And deserving," Gwen said. "You've earned it; you've paid your dues, Ellen, in addition to being loaded with talent. But that's enough of that. Don't want to swell your head. Speaking of earning, let's go spend some more of that whoppin' salary advance Dave gave you. Lady, you need clothes!"

A dozen times during the succeeding days Ellen had reason to thank Gwen for pushing her to get so many nice additions to her wardrobe. She was especially glad one night more than a week later. Rehearsal had ended early, and she'd come straight home to do her hair and nails. She'd had a light supper and put on a new blue gingham dress with a full skirt that made her feel like a kid who ought to swing and twirl and skip down the street. She was just about to leave the apartment, to treat herself to a movie, when there was a rap on the door.

Dave was leaning against the opposite wall, his head propped on his folded left arm, and his eyes staring intently as she opened the door. "Hiya," he said, straightening up, then moving across to stand right in front of her. "Stopped by to see if you want to go over to Printer's Alley with me for a while. We can drop in at Boots Randolph's, the Brass Rail, the Embers, whichever you want. How about it?"

Ellen's eyes went wide with surprise as she stepped back to let him enter the apartment. "Would you believe," she asked in little more than a whisper, "that I've never been to Printer's Alley?"

"You have to be kidding. That's one of the most busy, most visited places in old Music City, U.S.A."

"For tourists," she told him with a small smile, "and

for the likes of you, Mr. W., but not for a working gal so broke most of the time she couldn't afford an outing to the Hall of Fame!"

"Then let's do it. Powder your nose, grab your bag, whatever, and we'll gun over there." He moved past her into the shabby living room.

She felt a bubble of laughter well inside her. She twitched at the folds of her full skirt, shuffled her feet and winked at Dave. "I feel like a bird let out of a cage and dying to take off," she admitted.

"Then let's fly!"

And they did . . . to the heart of downtown Nashville. Printer's Alley was full of restaurants and nightclubs, accessible only on foot, along its narrow, twisting way. Ellen had seen it many times in passing, of course, but was thrilled to be one of the throng going in and out. Luckily, Dave had found a parking place not too far away, and they'd strolled arm in arm to the Alley, which bustled with gawking tourists. The sounds of country music filled the air. Bright neon signs flashed at the entertainment spots and Ellen, like the gawking tourists, stopped to stare.

"You're just like a hick come to town for the first time!" Dave laughed near her ear. "Which place would you like to try first?"

Ellen pointed toward the closest door. "Let's try the Embers Western Room. What I hear sounds great! You know me—I can't get enough of my favorite music." She found herself caught up in the excitement of the people coming and going and the twangy sound of gui-tars, fiddles and thumping drums. She pulled ahead of Dave to go inside, eager to experience whatever the place had to offer.

It was dark inside, and the mirrors lining the walls

made the room seem large. The place was filled with small tables, and at every one, shadowy figures sat sipping drinks. On the tiny stage in front of them, a blond-haired beauty in a form-fitting green gown with a plunging neckline was pouring out her heart in a song of tortured love; her voice, breaking with emotion, was backed by a band of guitars, drum and piano. A hostess, wearing a short-skirted outfit and a perky straw hat, led them to a table in the back and asked for their order.

"Just a wine cooler for me," Ellen said.

"Make mine a seven and seven," Dave told her. When the girl disappeared, Dave pulled a pair of horn-rimmed sunglasses from his pocket and slipped them on. "Just in case," he told her.

The drinks appeared almost instantly, and they sipped as they listened to the singer, a newcomer to the Nashville scene.

As Ellen's eyes grew accustomed to the darkened room, she noticed that it was much smaller than she had thought at first. The mirrors had been misleading. People came and people went. She and Dave sat through the show, listening to a quartet that patterned itself after the famous Oak Ridge Boys. On top of the table her fingers kept time to the music; under the table her feet were moving.

At the end of the set, Dave leaned across the table and said, "Want another drink, Ellen?"

She shook her head. "I'm nursing this one for a while, thanks. I want to show up for work in the morning with a clear head, you know. My boss is a tyrant."

Dave laughed and reached out to take her hand, bringing it to his lips to kiss the palm. "I'll tell him to go easy on you. Sometimes he listens to me. He's a moody guy. You'll have to bear with him. Actually, he's quite harmless."

Looking at Dave in the soft, intimate lighting, wearing the glasses, which didn't quite disguise his velvet-brown eyes, Ellen felt a warm glow engulf her. But not for an instant did she believe he was *harmless!*

The touch of his lips made a tingle run up the inside of her arm. She knew that with just a tiny bit of encouragement on her part, those gentle lips would smother her with kisses. Gentle kisses.

"Your eyes sparkle like opals in this light, Ellen. You look real lovely and sort of mysterious...the kind of lady I want to know through and through." The kiss he pressed into her wrist was stronger, more urgent.

Ellen shuddered with desire. But in spite of that feeling, she pulled her hand away, shaking her head.

"We're so great together when we sing, Dave. Do you think we ought to mess with such a good work partnership?"

"Work!" He snorted and rose abruptly, tossing bills onto the table. "Come on, woman, let's get out of here."

Dave led Ellen into the warm night air rippling down Printer's Alley—but the street had lost its color and charm for her. She let him guide her through the crowd filling the narrow street. They walked in silence, taking a roundabout route to the parked car, until suddenly Dave stopped and backed her against a brick wall.

"I know you're high as a kite about your singing, but don't go changing on me, Ellen McKay. I like you the way you are. Everybody else will, too. You have something very special...maybe part of it's your not having been around too much, your innocence."

She hooted. "Innocence! Dave, I was married to Carl on my eighteenth birthday and divorced over a year ago, just before my twenty-fourth. I'm down the road quite a ways from *innocence.*"

"I wasn't talking about sex. It's hard to explain—just

a special quality you have, kind of magical, and it shines like a light bulb when you sing. Maybe the words I want are *genuine* and *good-hearted*. Don't lose those, Ellen, ever." His voice was a husky whisper.

Tears started in her eyes, and she blinked hard. "You're so serious all of a sudden," she murmured. "Sorry if I caused the change. But Dave"—she looked at him pleadingly—"you're a big star, with so many hits that you probably don't even remember what it's like to want success. And . . . and it's just that at long last I feel able to let my dreams kind of take over for a little bit—"

"Aw, hon," he grumbled, pulling her close, "I don't want to stop you from dreaming." He hugged her hard, then pushed her an arm's length away. "I *do* remember the bad times. I got where I am the hard way, climbing up two rungs on the ladder and slipping back one." He frowned. "But all the while I was trying, I *lived*, too. I'm not now, never have been, *just* a musician. And I never let ambition take over my life."

Ellen bristled. "Are you accusing me of doing that?"

"Does the shoe pinch?"

She shook her head but said nothing. It might not quite pinch, but it sure was a tight fit.

"Let's move on." Dave took her arm and started in the direction of the car. "We'll get you home for your beauty sleep, princess. Not that you need it, mind." He planted a juicy kiss on her cheek, and even though they didn't talk much on the way back to her apartment, the mood between them was warmer . . . and building. The darkness encircling them in the coziness of the car banked the embers of their intimacy.

When Ellen stepped into the dimness of her living room and reached for the light switch on the wall, Dave's hand quickly shot out to restrain her. He turned her, taking her into the circle of his arms.

"We don't need lights, Ellen." His voice was husky as he kicked the door closed behind him. The street lights and the flashing red neon sign from a nearby gas station cast an eerie glow over them and the room.

Ellen shivered. "Dave, please, it's late." Her heart began pounding so fast at his nearness that she was sure he must feel it against his chest.

"I'm not leaving," he said, letting his lips caress her neck, her face. "Hell, woman, what was that 'work' stuff you were spouting?" he muttered into her hair, near her ear. "You're always on my mind. Just like I'm always on yours. Think I can't tell you want me? Think I don't see it, feel it everyday in the studio?"

She stifled a moan, then a laugh. "I'm that obvious?"

"That obvious."

Her arms went up to wrap around his neck, her hands losing themselves in the thickness of his hair and pulling his head down so their mouths met. Dave kissed her hungrily. His lips pressed hard against hers, then became more gentle, circling her mouth before tenderly catching her lips between his and sucking softly at them.

Ellen's nerve endings went crazy. She trembled under his tantalizing assault and strained closer to his hard, fit body. Her hands moved rhythmically over his back, fingers playing along his spine. They were both groaning, swaying, spellbound with need for each other.

He eased away and stared down at her. "You're a *very* desirable lady, my darlin', and don't think for a minute I'm going to say good night anytime soon." He led her by the hand to the couch, lowered himself onto it and then pulled her down on top of him.

"I could fall in love with you," he whispered, "if

you'd only give me half a chance."

"Oh, Dave, Dave," she cried softly.

"I want to make love to you right here and now."

Her own feelings were raging almost out of control, the ache of desire deep inside her clamoring for satisfaction. With her last bit of willpower, she muttered, "No, Dave—"

He raised his head and studied her face in the flickering neon light. "I don't believe that 'no,' Ellen. You want me as much as I want you. What's there to fight?" He cocked his head to the side, and she could see a scowl twisting his handsome features. "Unless you still have feelings for Carl..."

"Of course not!" She slid off him and sat on the edge of a cushion. Nervously she bowed over her knees and chewed at her bottom lip. "It's just such a hot and heavy thing between us so fast." She looked over her shoulder at him, then snapped her head back to stare around the strangely lighted room. "And I'm not a *fast* woman, Dave. There's only been Carl—"

She heard his angry hiss before she felt his hard fingers wrench her around so she was twisted at the waist and bent low to his face. "Don't you dare insult me or yourself by so much as hinting that what's between us is cheap! Woman, I ought to strangle you." He groaned, then laughed. "But all I want to do is love you to death!"

Then suddenly she was stretched out over the whole length of him and he was hugging her exuberantly, laughing like a child who's gotten everything on his Santa list. Kissing her hard, he wrapped his arms and legs around her body and together they rolled off the couch and onto the floor. His hands rubbed her back, his fingers finding the zipper of her dress and easing it down the length of her spine. He undressed her slowly between languorous kisses, until she was lying completely naked beneath his eyes.

"You're more beautiful than I imagined," he said hoarsely. His eyes took his fill of her, and she was completely unashamed. His lips lowered to her breast, the moistness and gentle suction of his mouth sending the honeyed agony of deep desire through her. His beard-roughened cheek moved over her soft skin to her taut belly and he circled her navel with his chin before returning to her other breast. Waves of thrilling sweetness washed through her.

"Dave, oh, Dave," she murmured. "I feel so . . . so wonderful. . . ."

"Half as wonderful as I feel?" he murmured in return. "Oh, woman, what I want to do to you!"

"Do it," she whispered urgently.

He began to work his magic with lips and tongue on her body. She'd never known this kind of slow lovemaking, and the rapture of it made her cry out over and over. When she could bear its exquisite pain and pleasure no longer, her hands went to Dave's shirt, practically ripping it away from his body. Her fingers circled his hard, flat nipples, teased the hair on his chest. She urged him to strip off his trousers and with a cry of abandon flung herself on him.

Their bare bodies strained into each other, writhing, then separating in a tantalizing play that made them wilder and wilder with need. Their bodies merged at the fever pitch of longing. And very soon Dave fufilled every promise of ecstasy that his lips, tongue, teeth and hands had made to her. She bit into his shoulder as her passion became explosive. She heard her strangled moans mingle with his hoarse cries as they crested together.

"My dear Lord," Dave said with fervor and reverence.

"Was there ever anything so beautiful?"

And those words made Ellen cry. Right then she could have died for love of Dave.

Some time in the middle of the night they moved to her narrow bed and made love again just as sweetly and then savagely as before, but with a new edge of desire that left Ellen stunned with happiness, with fulfillment.

Reluctantly she uncurled herself from the warm half-moon of Dave's body. The bedroom was brilliant with early-morning sunshine. She turned, propped her chin on her hand and looked down at him. He was wide awake, his soft brown eyes dancing with a smile of pure pleasure.

"Did anyone ever tell you that you are the champion kisser of the world, Mr. W.?"

He grinned up at her. "Got a crown to prove it."

Her right index finger circled his mouth. "Now if only music came out of here like those kisses," she taunted teasingly.

"Why, you vixen!" he said as he took the bait, popping up and rolling her over on her back, pinning her down. "Never make a slur against Dave Winston's music, lady, or you'll have to pay the consequences."

"Dave *who?*" she asked mischievously.

"That does it. *Consequences!*" He moved suggestively against her. "Hmm-m, don't know when we're ever going to get to that rehearsal, ma'am."

Chapter Seven

LENNY BURTON WAS the big name in Music City, just as he was all across the country. He appeared on stages from New York to Vegas, and for years Ellen had admired his work from afar. The middle-aged singer with his laid-back way of putting songs across proved that slow-and-easy ballads were still sure to sell. Lenny had been named Top Male Vocalist of the Year in Country Music two years in a row. Ellen was excited as she dressed in her new gown, feeling like Cinderella about to attend the palace ball. Her pumpkin coach was Dave's shiny Mercedes, and Dave, looking unbelievably handsome in his beige, custom-tailored Western suit, was her Prince Charming. It seemed too perfect, like a wonderful, exciting dream from which she would awaken at any moment.

They were companionably silent on the drive across town to Lenny's, on the banks of lovely Old Hickory Lake. His estate was well known, a place marked on tourist maps as a "must" for fans. Everything about the rambling stone mansion spelled elegance. The moment Ellen walked into the foyer on Dave's arm, she felt transformed and in another world. Crystal chandeliers, marble statues, thick oriental rugs, plush-covered and gilded furniture took her breath away, leaving her staring like an awestruck child. Servants glided around the room, carrying trays of crystal goblets filled with bubbling pink champagne or platters of fancy hors d'oeuvres. As more guests arrived, Ellen recognized the familiar faces of top country-music stars.

Lenny bounded over, stretching out his big hand. It glittered, and Ellen blinked. Every finger had a diamond ring jammed on it. He gave a lopsided grin of appreciation as he stared at Ellen.

"Lenny," Dave said, "I want you to meet my new vocalist, Ellen McKay. We're hoping for a chance to show off her talent tonight."

Ellen felt her face flame. Was Dave being too pushy? But Lenny's head bobbed in agreement so definite that he had to grab his hat to keep it from falling, and she instantly relaxed.

"Sure thing, Dave. I've heard a whisper or two around town that you've found yourself a real winner." He winked at Ellen. "A real pretty filly, for sure. Just don't let this guy hoodwink you, little lady. He can be a tough one to work with."

Ellen nodded, smiling at Lenny. "I'm finding that out."

Lenny studied her face a moment, the frown lines on his forehead deepening. "Say, aren't you married to Carl Kern?"

Ellen squared her slender shoulders. *"Was,* Lenny. That's past history. I'm my own woman again, and I'm loving it." She was incredibly grateful for Dave's warm, reassuring squeeze on her hand.

Lenny nodded understandingly. "I guess you know Carl is coming here tonight." He added, making it sound casual, "He's uninvited." Someone waved and called to him from across the room. He winked at Dave and Ellen. "I'll see you two later. That's Tom Springer over by the door. He's trying to hornswoggle me into some damn television thing he wants to do on Nashville. Them producers all have the hots for us Opry folks now." He laughed, a great booming set of guffaws. "And I remember a time not too long ago when they wouldn't touch us and our fans with a ten-foot pole. Far as they were concerned, every last one of us was either a hick or a hillbilly they looked down their noses at. How times *do* change."

"How they do!" Dave waved him off and turned back to Ellen. "Did you hear that, honey? A big-time producer in our midst."

"I heard," Ellen told him, looking across the room to catch a glimpse of the tall, bean-pole man wearing a tux. She turned back to face Dave. "But Lenny said Carl is coming here. He must have just arrived in town and said he'd crash the party. It sounds like something he might do." She shuddered. "I really don't want to see him, Dave."

A uniformed maid passed by with a tray of drinks, and Dave lifted two glasses from her tray. "After a few sips of the old bubbly, you won't mind facing your ex. You're going to have to meet up with him sooner or later, Ellen. Nashville isn't that big a town, and Carl comes and goes."

Ellen sipped her champagne, staring at the people

milling about the room. It seemed a good time to bring up something that had been bothering her. "I've heard that you know him, Dave. Why didn't you tell me that yourself?" She scowled, feeling thwarted as a tall, willowy, raven-haired woman wearing black gaucho pants and boots and a flaming orange blouse approached them, her crimson lips easing into a toothpaste-ad smile.

"Dave Winston," she purred. "You darling! How are you? I haven't seen you in months and months. Not since that filming party at Opryland, in fact." She looked Dave up and down. "You look handsomer than ever."

"Thanks, Marg." Dave flashed her a grin and kissed her lightly on the cheek before turning to introduce her to Ellen. "You've read Marg Janner's daily gossip column, I'm sure. Everyone in Music City starts the day with Marg."

Ellen nodded, swallowing another sip of champagne before smiling at the reporter. "Of course. I wouldn't miss your column, Miss Janner. It keeps me up on the local comings and goings."

The heavily mascaraed lashes blinked as Marg Janner appraised Ellen's trim figure. "I try," she said sweetly. "And you must be Dave's new backup singer. . . ."

"Ellen McKay," Dave told her. "Remember that name, Marg. It's going to be on everyone's lips after tonight."

The woman's penetrating eyes studied Ellen's face as though searching for a flaw in her subtle make-up. Ellen sipped at her drink, feeling decidedly uncomfortable, clear to the toes of her sandals, then happily relieved when Dave came to her rescue. "This gal is a terrific talent, Marg. We'll be doing a duet or two later on, and I'm sure she'll raise a few eyebrows."

Marg nodded, still staring at Ellen. "I'll have to mention you in tomorrow's write-up," she said, managing a weak smile before moving away to join another group of guests sipping cocktails nearby.

The crowd grew in size, and Gwen appeared with her date, a middle-aged banker she introduced as Sam Cord. They pushed their way to where Ellen and Dave stood. The patio doors were opened, encouraging people in the crowded room to move outside to the lantern-lit gardens. The evening was warm and clear, and Ellen and Gwen left the men talking with friends while they walked around the grounds, speaking briefly to other guests. They went to the front of the mansion, where guests were still arriving.

"I really like to watch the cars arrive. I thought you might enjoy the sight, too," Gwen told Ellen. "Have you ever seen so many white Cadillacs in one place? And look at that Rolls over there! Guess who that belongs to?"

Ellen's eyes roamed the circular driveway, where many of the automobiles were parked. A shiny, yellow Rolls Royce stood apart from the rest, impossible to ignore.

"I wouldn't dare guess. There are so many big names here tonight. It could belong to any one of them," Ellen answered, shaking her head.

Gwen laughed. "Let me enlighten you. It belongs to Lenny himself. He parks it there for show. He's quite a guy. Sounds down-home and sometimes simple, but he's a real shrewd character, who enjoys every cent he makes. He owns five cars! Two Caddies, the Rolls, a Jaguar and an M.G. He has a private jet, *and* out there on the lake he keeps a yacht that looks like a small version of the *Queen Elizabeth!*"

Ellen was about to comment when a taxi pulled up

at the front door and let out a tall man wearing a light-blue Western suit. There was a bright-blue feather in his cowboy hat. He paid the driver and turned toward the house, pausing a moment to look up at the columns on the portico. The lights illuminated the walk, and Ellen gasped, stepping quickly back into the shadows of the garden trees.

"That's Carl!" she whispered hoarsely. "Oh, Gwen . . . I don't want to see him! Why did he have to come here, of all places? I hadn't heard from him since our divorce; then he phoned me the other day from California. I hung up on him." Her voice was rough with anxiety, and Gwen put a comforting arm around her shoulders.

They walked back toward the patio, where a country-music band was playing a lively novelty song made famous by Mac Davis. Sam and Dave were standing near the shimmering pool with another man and a woman. They seemed totally engrossed in conversation when Ellen and Gwen joined them, but Dave was thoughtful enough to interrupt and introduce them, owners of a big record shop in town. Ellen tried to join the conversation, but her mind was on Carl's arrival. With luck he might remain inside the house or miss seeing her in the crowd. He would hear her sing later with Dave, but there was nothing she could do about that.

Dave got her mind off Carl by starting to circulate, making sure she met dozens of people from disc jockeys to superstars. Her head was dizzy from trying to remember names to put together with faces in the future. Press agents roamed among the guests, along with TV and recording-studio executives. Ellen was spellbound. These were the people she had dreamed of meeting for years, the people who make the stars or break them. She made certain to wear her most dazzling smile and be charming.

The music was good, mostly country, but with a disco tune thrown in every now and then for variety. After an hour of cocktails, dancing began, and couple after couple made their way to the specially constructed dance area at the far end of the lantern-lit patio. The fiddles became muted, playing slow, country-style waltzes. Dave set his drink aside, excused them from the group they had been talking with and led Ellen to the dance floor.

"I've been waiting for an excuse to take you in my arms for almost two hours," he whispered in her ear.

"Needing an excuse is new for you, I can tell." She smiled broadly, then nestled against him, resting her head on his shoulder and drifting to the music. His hands slid to her lower back, pinning her tighter against him as they danced. The embers smoldered, sparked, blazed into searing flame as Dave's lips teased her ear. She pulled back and looked up at him, her eyes dreamy with desire.

"You are a dangerous man, Dave," she whispered. "It must be the champagne...and the magic of this party...but I'm getting wild ideas. I'll be Scarlet and you be Rhett. There's a winding staircase inside that goes up to fabulously furnished bedrooms."

"I'll rent or borrow this place from Lenny sometime, and we'll play *Gone with the Wind* till we can't anymore. But frankly, my dear—"

She laughed hard at his drawling imitation of Clark Gable.

"Yes, frankly, my dear," he went on, "right now our host wants our attention."

Lenny Burton appeared on the platform, raising his hands to stop the dancing. His hat was pushed back, showing a fringe of black curly hair streaked with gray, and his face was flushed from too many cocktails. He swayed slightly, grabbing the microphone for support.

"Hey, gang... I think it's about time we had some local talent... how about it?" His words were just a little slurred. "What do you say we make a few of these dead-beats sing for their supper?"

A round of applause answered his question. Guests flocked from inside the mansion to crowd around the pool, everyone eager for a show of talent.

"Dave Winston's here with a gorgeous little gal on his arm whom he'd like to introduce to y'all." Lenny's bloodshot eyes searched the throng. "Hey, Dave, old buddy, are you out there? Git your bones up here."

Ellen felt Dave tighten his grip on her hand and move up behind Lenny from the dance floor. She swallowed hard. This was it! Tomorrow, Nashville would either approve of her or—she shut off her thoughts. Right now it didn't matter what followed that "or."

"Dave... I'm not sure," she muttered, her voice shaky.

He squeezed her hand for reassurance. "I am, honey. Let's knock 'em dead. We can do it."

The shouts and whistles showed how well liked Dave Winston was among his fellow musicians in the town so overflowing with talent. Ellen had a feeling this was going to be a repeat of that dream she'd had after first meeting Dave. If she appeared alone, those big names staring at them now would throw mushy grapes her way. But with Dave supporting her talent, they would listen. They would make their judgments... but they *would* listen.

"Hey, gang," Dave greeted the crowd, smiling his widest and waving his free hand. "Meet my new part-ner... Ellen McKay. Ellen McKay," he repeated, louder. Remember that name. You're going to hear it a lot from now on." He leaned over to plant a firm kiss on her flushed cheek. There were raucous calls and applause. Dave quieted them with an upraised hand. "We're going to do a couple of songs now that I plan to add to my new album. And we'll do them at the Opry again tomorrow night."

He leaned over to talk to the band, and the music started. Ellen was relieved when his arm encircled her waist, giving her the support she needed. Her knees felt like jello and quaked as badly. But her fears miraculously left her as their voices blended perfectly in the softly haunting duet. The ballad was one she enjoyed singing, and she completely forgot the audience as she slowly became part of the music. When the first song ended, they went right into the second before applause could break in. It was a livelier, hand-clapping song of a lost love rediscovered.

The weakness in Ellen's knees returned as the last notes faded and the crowd remained absolutely silent. She felt herself swallow hard, a numbness sweeping her. Dave tightened his grip around her waist just as all hell broke. Shouts of "More..." "Encore..." "Give us another" greeted them. Ellen looked up at Dave, unbelieving, laughing. "Do they like me?" she muttered, incredulous.

His laugh was deep, excited. "I'd sure say so. Shall we do another?" He pulled her close, his lips touching her forehead. "You're *in* now, my darlin'."

When the noise quieted to a murmur, Dave spoke into the mike. "Any requests?"

"How about 'First Time Heartache, Second Time Love'?" a man's voice shouted. The audience agreed, applauding and whistling.

Ellen glanced up at Dave, her doubts mounting. "I'm not sure about that one. We haven't practiced it . . ."

His grin was confident as he winked at her. "We can do it. That oughta be *our* song, and besides, we're on a roll, Ellen. Nothing can stop us now."

She sighed, wishing that at this moment she could steal his faith. Everything had gone so well up to now, she would hate to end the performance with a dull thud. If that happened, eagle-eyed, open-eared Marg Janner would certainly make the most of it in her morning column.

The band played the slow introduction to the haunting love song, with quiet guitars and soft fiddles leading into their entrance. She looked up at Dave, her eyes mirroring her anxiety. When he winked at her again, she took the cue and let her voice join his in their very special blending. As the last notes faded, Ellen dared to look out at the crowd. She could see it on their faces! They were excited, as if they had been let in on a very special happening! A feeling of pride welled up inside her. Heaven knows, she had worked long and hard for this moment. She relaxed and blew the audience a kiss, smiling her thanks and bowing her head as she and Dave stepped off the platform. From inside the group standing nearest to them, a tall man staggered forward.

"Howdy, love of my life. You look good enough to take up to bed. Want to—for old time's sake? I promised you satin sheets, remember? Old Len has them on every bed. I checked it out."

Ellen's smile vanished, and a cold shiver went up her spine. The silence around the pool was unbearable, and then there was a low murmur, which began to spread. Ellen felt a knot growing inside her, pushing its way upward to lodge in her throat, stifling her. Her face burned with color. She kept her head lowered, wanting to have the floor open and swallow her up.

"Carl, how could you?" she gasped, fighting tears. Dave tightened his grip on her, turning to the band. "How about a song, guys?..." He turned to Carl. "Move on, buddy," he said firmly, and Carl staggered back and made his way inside, grinning and mumbling about satin sheets and pink champagne.

The music became loud, and the embarrassed guests milled about, chattering, some returning to the floor to dance, others returning to the lavishly-laid-out buffet table inside the mansion. The incident was brushed aside, forgotten.

Dave led Ellen to a quiet corner, brushing away her tears gently with his thumbs. "Hey...it's all right, Ellen." His voice was quiet. "Carl's a heel, and everyone here knows it. Forget him. We were a hit, and everyone loves you."

The tears burned Ellen's eyes again. "I could die!" She sniffed. "I've never been so embarrassed in my life. Oh, Dave...I want to go home...please."

He shook his head. "Not now, honey. There's a big TV producer headed our way. Smile..." He traced her quivering lips with his finger. "Remember the old corny slogan...the show must go on.... And if you forget that, just remember I'm crazy about you and not going to move from your side."

She sniffed, and he pulled a handkerchief out of his pocket and handed it to her. "Better hurry," he warned. "He's closing in fast. Ten yards...five yards..." She blew her nose, giggling at Dave's rundown, feeling her tensions ease. "OK, boss, I'll behave," she whispered, "but I must look a sight...."

He kissed the tip of her nose, quickly stuffing the handkerchief into his back pocket and shaking his head. "No way, honey...no way."

*   *   *

"I don't believe what just happened!" Ellen exclaimed, shaking her head as she watched the TV producer ease his way into a group standing near the small poolside bar. "That man just offered us a guest appearance on TV! Pinch me! I have to make sure I'm awake and in my right mind."

Dave's laugh was hearty. "I'll kiss you instead," he told her. "I'm not in the habit of pinching pretty ladies." He let his lips slide gently along her neck, nibbling at an especially vulnerable spot. She shivered with pleasure. "You're awake, honey, don't worry about that." He smiled at her, looking very pleased. "He certainly did put it to us, made us one of those offers you can't refuse."

She nodded. "But I can't believe it! Everything is happening so fast, Dave. I'm numb. Here I am about to sing at the Opry tomorrow night and getting a chance to sing on TV." She shook her head, unbelieving, then sighed. "I have to admit, I like the way I'm feeling. My confidence is building by leaps and bounds."

He nodded. "I can see that." His tone was suddenly serious, Ellen noted. The look on his face was hard for her to read. If she didn't know better or wasn't feeling so excited, she might think his eyes mirrored concern.

Lenny moved through the chatting guests to the platform, grabbing the microphone to shout, "Time for someone else to sing for his supper. How about you, Johnny Frank? Get your lanky bones and six-string up here and give us a tune."

Ellen and Dave moved closer when the tall, pencil-thin Johnny trotted up onto the stage. "I want to hear him," Ellen exclaimed. "I just bought his new *Frank Live* album. It's terrific!"

"Not bad," Dave agreed.

Johnny Frank began to strum his guitar in a slow, lazy way, and after a long introduction, broke into a wailing song of prison woes and the woman who'd done him wrong.

The entertainment continued at well-spaced intervals, with every known name at the party taking a turn on stage. Between numbers, Dave and Ellen made their way to the table, laden with food ranging from salad to shrimp, chicken, ham, roast beef, and mouth-watering desserts. They served themselves generously and found a bench in a secluded corner of the patio to enjoy their meal. Gwen and Sam joined them, then several of the other guests.

The evening was almost too exciting. Ellen enjoyed talking with the stars she had never met before. All the people she spoke to, without exception, congratulated her, saying how much they enjoyed her singing, and congratulated Dave on finding her. Ellen felt as if she'd drunk too much champagne, or maybe it was the combination of the compliments and the drinks, but her head felt light, as if she were moving through a dreamworld featuring fancy outfits, designer gowns and expensive cars.

Even the sight of Carl weaving toward her at a second when she was off by herself didn't disturb her as it would have earlier in the evening. He carried a glass of champagne in each hand, sipping first one, then the other. He paused in front of her, looking down with a scowl.

"You could be more friendly, Ellen. We did have a lot of good times, you know. Don't let your success go to your head, baby. It can fade overnight." He gave a snort of disgust. "What a life." He grinned at her. "We sure had a lot of fun, you and me. And we made a hell of a lot of good love, remember?"

Ellen drew in her breath, squaring her shoulders as she looked up at him. "Carl, our marriage is ancient history," she told him quietly. "I have a new life now; let me live it. You found success—now it's my turn."

His stocky body swayed as he narrowed his eyes and leaned down closer to her. The champagne sloshed in the glasses. "I want you to sing with *me*, Ellen. Things ain't going too well lately. But if you sang with me, I know I could hit the charts. Your voice is terrific now."

Dave had come up just in time to hear Carl's last remarks. "Hit the road, Mac. She's with me."

Carl shook his head, waving one hand in the air, splashing the drink. "You don't need her . . . I need her. Nobody wants my act anymore . . ." He swayed toward Ellen, and the champagne slopped all over her skirt. She jumped up and ran to the house, hurrying through to the powder room. Gwen followed her.

A pert, uniformed maid sat primly inside the multi-mirrored room, ready to be of help to the guests. She immediately produced a cloth and cleaning fluid and went down on her knees to sponge the damp spots on the gown. Ellen's eyes brimmed with tears of anger and humiliation. Her entire body trembled as she fought to catch her breath. Gwen, her help not needed, stood by, watching as the young woman wiped the frothy material with the cleaning fluid before she turned a hair dryer on the damp spots. It took almost a half hour of sponging and rubbing and drying before Gwen and the maid stood back and pronounced the dress fine. Ellen stared down at it, smoothing her skirt to see for herself if any telltale traces of Carl's mishap remained.

"It looks like new," Gwen said, cocking her head and squinting. "I'd never know that accident happened."

The maid nodded. "It isn't at all noticeable, Miss McKay. Thank goodness it was only champagne."

Ellen nodded, smiling at the attractive maid, feeling good because the young woman had recognized her, knew her name. How many others would know her now, or soon, when she appeared in public? she wondered.

"Thank you . . ." Ellen reached into her beaded handbag, ready to give the girl a tip for her help.

"Oh, no, Miss McKay! I couldn't take anything. I'm just pleased that I was able to help. Your gown is much too lovely to have it ruined by some drunk." She looked disgusted, then sheepish. "A lady came in here just before you did, and mentioned what happened. I didn't know it was you! I heard you and Dave Winston sing earlier, and I loved it. You have a terrific voice. If you have an album soon, I'll buy it for sure."

Ellen felt her tensions ease. Gwen laughed. "Hear that? You're on your way to fame and fortune, as the old saying goes."

"I hope so," Ellen exclaimed. "But I certainly don't need people like Carl Kern trying to sabotage my way there."

They went back to join the others, and found everything was peaceful on the patio. Dave and Sam stood talking to Johnny Frank and his wife, Kelly, a willowy redhead wearing orange lipstick and a bright-green dress to match her name. Dave turned to Ellen, looking concerned.

"Are you OK?"

"Sure . . . fine." She kept her voice low and gave him a tiny wry smile.

"Lenny asked Carl to leave," Dave told her, then remembered. "Hey . . . you haven't met Johnny and Kelly yet."

Johnny Frank leaned down to plant a kiss on her forehead. "Welcome to the inner circle, little gal," he told her. "I do think old Dave has picked himself some kind of a partner. I hope he has brains enough to hang onto you."

"Johnny, you're embarrassing her." Kelly's warm Texas drawl was a whisper.

Ellen laughed. "Don't worry, after tonight, I won't embarrass easily anymore. I'm sure happy to meet you two. Johnny, I've got stacks of your records at home."

Johnny shoved his Western hat back and tipped his head, laughing heartily. "Now, *that's* what I like to hear! I'll sure buy yours, little filly, the minute they hit the record stores."

"I think you're pulling my leg a bit, but I love it." Ellen laughed.

She saw Dave's frown and winked at him. "Don't look so glum, Dave."

He shook his head. "I do believe I have created a monster to come back and haunt me."

"Never," she assured him.

The party continued far into the night, finally breaking up just a couple of hours before the early-morning birds would create competition for the musicians. One by one, the "beautiful people" of Music City piled into their Cadillacs and assorted shiny chariots and drove off into the sunrise. Ellen savored every last minute, hating to see it end. Reluctantly, at last she slipped into Dave's car for the ride back to her apartment. She leaned her head back against the seat, her eyes closed. It had been fabulous, an important night. Dave seemed to sense her need to dream and sort out the events of the night. He didn't speak until they were almost at her apartment, then he glanced at her.

"Think you'll feel up to rehearsal today? We have to go over the Opry songs."

She turned her head, stretching and yawning. "Oh, Dave, did you have to burst the bubble? I've been sailing up there in the clouds, hating to come back to earth."

He shook his head, laughing. "Sorry, but all good things must come to an end."

He pulled up in front of her apartment, switched off the ignition and turned on the seat to face her, leaning close. "I'm glad you enjoyed yourself tonight. I thought it would be good for you to meet some of those people and for them to hear you. Contacts are important, and make no mistake, Ellen, the wheels are in motion. You won't be able to turn back now, even if you want to."

She drew in a deep, luxurious breath, her lips curved in a self-satisifed smile. "I don't want to, Dave. I love it!" She closed her eyes, half expecting him to take her in his arms.

Dave sighed, turning back to strum his fingers on the steering wheel thoughtfully. "Too bad Carl had to show up," he said, "although I thought you handled him well."

She sat up and looked him in the eye, unblinking. "Did you talk to Carl after you hired me?"

Dave gave an almost inaudible little snort and nodded. "You want to know about Carl and me, of course. Well, we met at that big country-western jamboree up in the hills in New York State last summer, and he asked my advice about his new group. He mentioned you and how you had knocked the pins out from under him when you divorced him. He said his career hadn't been doing well since then, because he couldn't forget you. He also said you were a good singer and only needed a chance to prove it. So, when I saw your name at the audition, then heard you sing, I decided Carl was right, and wanted to give you that chance. I called him to let him know I'd hired you." He looked away, staring across the street at a dim streetlamp. Then he turned back to face her. "Does that answer all your questions?"

She looked at him, thinking how tired, how drained, he looked. But she had to continue. "In other words, I owe the break you've given me to Carl? At least in part?"

As he reached over to take her hand, she tried to pull away. He held it fast, bending his head to kiss her fingers. "Don't you know I would have chosen you anyway, honey, even if I hadn't heard your name from Carl? Look, I think right now you're just plain tired. I know I am, and the effects of that pink champagne are fading fast. Go in and get some sleep, and come to the studio at noon."

She stiffened, tossing her luxurious mane of hair back off her shoulders.

"Don't be angry. If I haven't mentioned Carl, it's because I didn't think you wanted to be reminded of him." He shrugged, holding out his hands, palms up, in a quick gesture. "That's it, I swear." He offered her a faint crooked smile. "Truce?"

She nodded, but she thought she glimpsed a strange, almost cynical expression flickering briefly in his dark eyes; then it vanished, and the cocky, infectious grin returned. "Sleep tight, for a few hours, anyway..."

Chapter Eight

ELLEN'S SUBCONSCIOUS REFUSED to give up and make peace with her exhausted body. She tossed and turned, twisting the bedcovers into knots around her legs.

Long sandy strips of beach stretched for miles ahead of her. Blue ocean waters swept a gentle surf ashore. She walked barefoot, clad in jogging shorts and a clinging T-shirt, the breeze, salty and damp, ruffling her hair. The waves washed over her feet, melting the wet sand under them. She stopped, letting her feet sink until the sand squished between her toes. And she laughed, feeling free, and happier than she had ever been before. A man walked toward her, dressed in bright-red swimming trunks. His bronze skin glistened with drops of ocean water as he drew nearer. She tried to run to him, but the surf became rougher, holding her back.

"Dave," she called, holding out her arms.

He waved and broke into a run, covering the distance to her in long, jogging strides. When he reached her, his arms encircled her, holding her against him in a tight, crushing embrace. His open mouth found hers, and she returned his hungry kisses. Her body shivered with desire.

"Oh, Dave," she moaned. "I love you, I love you..."

His kisses moved down, sampling the tender spot in the hollow of her throat, then trailing fire to the lobe of one ear, then the other.

"Ellen," he whispered hoarsely, pulling her down onto the wet sand. The cool water splashing over them raised her nipples under her clinging T-shirt. Dave pushed it up until her firm round breasts were bare, and he raised himself on his arms, looking down at her, his eyes smoldering with desire. "You're so beautiful," he whispered, bending to kiss one firm breast, then the other. Ellen drew in her breath, her whole body wanting him, needing him.

The wave rolled in, big and dark and frightening, engulfing them in the salty, foamy surge as they lay in a tight embrace on the sand. Ellen pulled away. She jumped to her feet, sputtering for breath, her hair matted and dripping, her clothes clinging to her body.

"There isn't any ocean surf in Nashville," she exclaimed, shaking her head at the man still stretched out at her feet.

He stood up, facing her, his dark hair hanging in a wet thatch on his forehead. "We're on tour," he told her, reaching out his arms. "We said we'd make love morning, noon and night on tour."

She shook her head, backing away. "I have to go back to work now. I have to rehearse, then perform."

He pulled her close. "To hell with your career. I love you, Ellen McKay."

Their tanned, wet bodies came together in an embrace. Ellen reached up to push the damp hair from his forehead, laughing. "And I love you, Dave. You're right! To hell with my career. . . ."

She turned in bed, the moaning sound of her anguish waking her. For a while she remained quiet, her eyes closed, remembering the dream. It had been so very real, her body still tingled as if Dave had made love to her. The dream had shaken her, but she remembered her mother's words of wisdom years earlier when a particular nightmare had frightened her. "Dreams are *contrary*, Ellen Patricia. They are *never* real." Maybe so, but the one she had just slept through certainly *felt* real.

The rehearsal wasn't one of the best. Dave was in a bad mood, and nothing seemed to go right. It wasn't that *she* triggered his annoyance, she noted. This time it seemed to be every *other* one in the group who drew his wrath. Tom sang off-key during a brief humming solo; Red's timing was off in a lead-in. Gwen interrupted in the middle of their duet with an important phone call from Dave's publicity agent, and the rehearsal was set back while he took the lengthy call in his office.

Dave had arrangements to make, and Ellen was glad to be alone and to relax until it was time to head for the Opry. That thought set up waves of protest in the pit of her stomach. It was a country singer's dream about to come true. Everyone wanted a crack at singing at the Grand Ole Opry. Just the thought of appearing on stage with the greats like Roy Acuff made her tingle with anticipation. She would be singing backup, with the exception of the one song Dave had chosen for their duet.

It had sounded good to her in rehearsal, in spite of Dave's doubts, his concern that they weren't up to their standard.

As usual, the Grand Ole Opry was sold out. Even in the days when the show rang the rafters at the Ryman Auditorium, overflowing the old church pews and stifling in the heat of Nashville's summers, Ellen knew that Grand Ole Opry had been the city's biggest attraction. People traveled for miles to attend a show, to see their favorite stars right before their eyes. There was a certain magic to each performance. It seemed spontaneous, as if there'd been no rehearsing. And there was always that wonderful excitement of just *being* there where the action moved around you.

Ellen had been there many times to view the shows, dreaming of one day walking onto the stage. It seemed to her to be the very ultimate for a country-western singer. The Opry spelled success, the top of the ladder. She felt a thrill entering the Opry for the first time through the stage door. Stagehands, lighting director, stage manager, engineers and the staff band were ready for the opening curtain. Dave was busy chatting with the announcer who was to handle the first half-hour of the show. Performers milled about, talking, warming up, tuning instruments and waiting for the show to begin. Dave waved to Ellen as she stepped over props and made her way to join him near the many ropes used to raise and lower various backdrops.

"Hi," she greeted him, smiling. "I made it!"

Dave kissed her and introduced her to the announcer, who made a casual remark about being glad to meet her but quickly moved on to talk to the MC for the first segment.

"When will we go on?" Ellen asked Dave.

He was busy now, tuning up his guitar, and she wondered if he was put out with her or just down and a little nervous. His coolness that day had seemed odd to her, but now, standing close to him, watching him deftly finger the six-string guitar, leaning his head close to hear the cords, her excitement at just being at the famous Opry seemed heightened because of him and his musicianship. Satisfied with the sound of his guitar, he turned his attention to her.

"We come on late in the first half of the show. It's a good spot. We won't have time to worry about it . . . If you're worried."

She drew in a deep breath, watching the bustle around her. "Of course I'm worried! I'm scared to death!"

He gave her a strange smile. "Why should you be scared? It's my show, honey." He used the endearing word a bit flippantly, she thought, and it stung like a slap in the face.

"I know that, Dave. But, it's my first time on this stage. Don't you see, it's like walking on hallowed ground. My goodness . . . and here I am standing here, too! The very thought gives me goose bumps."

He laughed aloud. "Don't worry about it. I'll bet by the last note of our duet you'll have every one of those forty-four hundred people out there in the audience eating out of your hand and crying for more. . . ."

Why did she have the feeling he wasn't too keen on that idea? Something was bothering Dave, something that was eroding the warmth and joy between them. Whatever it was, she knew that if they weren't careful, it could also erode that magic blending of their voices. That mustn't happen! And this night—at least—it didn't. They were beautiful together.

When the final "So long for now!" echoed through the Opry building and the final curtain fell, the crowd filed out into the cooling night air. The performers packed their instruments, talking among themselves, some ready to head for home to rest their tired bodies, others still wide enough awake to want to drive to the Alley for drinks or stop at Boots's place just to hear his mellow sax and unwind. Dave's Greyhounds left the building as soon as their half-hour stint on stage ended. Ellen felt too high to go home. She wanted to remain, to savor each moment . . . the atmosphere, the cheering audience, the smell of popcorn permeating the building, the flashing bulbs from dozens of cameras. Every bit of the evening was dazzling to her, and she wanted to remember the tiniest detail.

Dave seemed pleased at their reception from the crowd. The applause had been like a symphony to Ellen's ears. It kept up until they gave the audience an encore, one of the songs they had sung together at Lenny's party the night before. But it wasn't quite the same. Ellen felt it the moment she left the backup group to stand beside Dave for their song. He kept his distance, not moving so close as he had previously, not letting his strong arm tighten to give her reassurance during those first scary notes on the Opry stage.

Dave had gone off with Rocky on business, and the last members of the stage crew were finishing their chores for the night when Ellen finally left the theater and walked across the vast parking lot to her car. She stood for a moment looking at the Opry building, standing like a guard at the entrance to Opryland. How could she ever explain to anyone just what this night had meant to her? With the possible exception of Dave's change in attitude toward her, it had been perfect, an evening to be kept filed in her memory, to remember again and again.

She was still high with excitement as she drove across

Nashville to her apartment. To unwind, she drove a long, twisting route, which took her past the old red brick Ryman Auditorium. Now, after appearing on the Opry stage, she wondered what it had been like back in the 1940s, when the Opry moved into the Ryman, after various homes since its beginning in 1925. She had gone there once, years ago, with Carl, to walk over the creaking floors, breathe in the musty odors of the past, and she had taken delight in standing on the spot in center stage where so many of the old greats had stood when they performed. It had made her tingle just to think of being where ghosts of Tex Ritter, Hank Williams and others probably still kept watch. The old church pews had been hard and uncomfortable, and the air in the building was stifling. Only true lovers of country-western music would have endured stiff backs and perspiring brows for hours to watch the shows there. Now, at least, the Opry fans sat on carpeted pews and listened to their favorites perform in air-conditioned comfort.

Finally ready to face her dreary apartment, Ellen turned toward home. She parked in front of the building, because it was easier and because two lights were out in the parking lot and she wasn't eager to tempt muggers. Her spirits were high when she stopped in front of her door, the key in her hand. The door stood partway open, and she recognized the guitar music filtering out into the dimly lit hallway as being on one of the many tapes in her Chet Atkins collection. For a moment, she stood listening for some other sound, not wanting to enter the room, already certain who was waiting for her inside. Before she could move, the door opened wide, and Carl's chiseled features broke into an arrogant smile. He looked very relaxed, shirt sleeves rolled high and top buttons open, showing a gold medallion glistening against the dark mat of hair curling on his chest.

"Hi, angel."

Ellen brushed past him into the room, her anger mounting by the second. "How did you get in here, Carl?"

He closed the door behind her and stood watching her as she tossed her beaded purse onto the coffee table and sat down to fumble for a cigarette in the china box on the table. Carl hurried over to her, pulling a silver lighter from his back pocket and leaning down to light her cigarette.

His arrogant grin remained pasted on his face. "That's easy. The janitor remembered me the minute I told him my name. I told him I had to see you on important business, so he let me in to wait for you. I was over at the Black Poodle in the Alley, and I picked up a paper on my way out and saw your rave notice, so I came to congratulate you. Don't worry—I'm OK, Ellen... sober as one of your new boyfriend's dogs." He laughed. "I had time for a few cups of black coffee and a shower while I waited for you."

She inhaled and let the smoke drift from her nostrils. She had nothing to say to Carl, and she was stewing over his invasion of her privacy.

He sat down on a chair across from her, drumming his fingers nervously on the chair arm. "Have you read the paper today? You stomped your way right up the hill here in Music City, angel. I figured I'd better see you while you're still speaking to us low-down hillbillies."

There was bitterness in his voice that Ellen couldn't miss. She kicked off her shoes and put her feet up on the coffee table, leaning back to wait for him to go on, too tired now to put up an argument about his presence.

When he didn't continue, she shook her head, sighing.

"I don't know what you're talking about, Carl."

"Sure, you do. You're no bubble-brain, like some of the gals I've sung with. Listen, El, you can see I've got a problem...I mean, I drink more than I should. The crowd I've been traveling with since we split is on a permanent roller coaster. I've missed a few performances and had a few others pulled out from under me. In other words, I'm falling low and I see the bottom comin' up. To be honest, I need a new break...and I think you're it." He leaned toward her, his eyes appraising her slender, well-formed legs and traveling up to her bare shoulders. "I haven't forgotten how great we were together, El. I don't think you have either. We could start out just singing together. Then"—he shrugged—"who knows?"

Ellen swung her legs down, slipped her sandals on and leaned forward to crush out her cigarette. She stood up, shaking her head in disbelief. "You have to be kidding, Carl. Our marriage was a bigger disaster than the Johnstown flood. I'm not about to try for a repeat on *that!* Look, if you put in a word for me with Dave, I'm grateful, but aside from that, I don't owe you a thing." She winced, softening to Carl's plight. But quickly she reminded herself of all she'd done for this man, sacrificing and suffering to help him find success. Hoarse and low, she said, "I've paid my dues in those crummy little two-bit road houses long enough, Carl. I want to work for Dave, to learn from him."

Carl got up, moving toward her, swaying slightly. He made a grab for her, and she moved back.

"You're still not sober," she snapped. "Get out, Carl. Just leave me alone. And don't try this enter-and-make-yourself-at-home trick again."

This time his hand grabbed her wrist, and he pulled her roughly to him. Almost savagely, he reached up to weave his fingers in her hair, pulling her head back and kissing her hungrily.

"I'm not leaving," he growled against her throat. "I need you, El. Damn it, you *do* owe me, and I'm going to collect."

She struggled, using every ounce of her strength to try to break free. "You're hurting me," she told him, moving her head to avoid his bruising mouth. Her scalp was tingling from his grasp on her hair, and she could feel tears of anger and pain filling her eyes. The smell of whiskey made her stomach churn. Carl continued to hold her, pulling her head still further back until she cried out. His unshaven face rubbed against her throat, and in that moment she kicked out, her shoe finding his shin. He pulled his hand out of her hair, jumping back.

Ellen ran to the door and opened it. "Get out!" she cried, fighting tears.

Carl snatched his jacket off the chair and, subdued now, looked sheepish as he went into the hall. "I'm sorry..." he muttered as he passed her. "I still love you, El...."

She slammed the door, locking it immediately and sliding the chain into place as a double precaution. She was trembling now, still breathless from the encounter with Carl. It was not the end she had wanted for the wonderful evening she had just lived through at Grand Ole Opry. She felt weak and drained, afraid and confused by Carl's reentry into her life. And Dave. She wanted him... needed him... and not tomorrow, but now!

"Damn!" she exclaimed, kicking her shoes across the room. One landed on the couch, the other in front of the kitchen door. "I should have known, whenever something good happens, something bad usually follows close behind," she muttered angrily; then, shaking her head, she laughed. "Listen to you, Ellen McKay, talking to yourself. Time for a shower and bed. The world will look brighter in the morning."

Dave was out of town. It was the Saturday exactly one week after the performance at the Opry. Ellen slept late, then spent the remainder of the day on chores she had put aside for far too long. She crammed a load of clothes into the washing machine in the basement, cleaned her apartment, shampooed her luxurious hair, manicured her nails, wrote checks to cover monthly bills, and finally relaxed to read a romance she had begun weeks earlier. She had promised herself a lazy, "catching-up" day. Too much had happened in a short time. She had begun to feel like a spinning top, wanting to unwind but not knowing how.

The long, work-filled days after Lenny's party and following her exciting Opry appearance had been nerve-wracking. Dave had called for several extra rehearsals, anxious to make sure the group was polished to perfection for its recording session and the fast-approaching road tour. The rehearsals of old, with Aggie serving coffee and tasty refreshments, were definitely a thing of the past. Dave had become even more of a taskmaster, demanding nothing short of perfection from each of his band members and backup singers, not letting up until he'd gotten that perfection. The sessions became more and more exhausting, leaving Ellen's nerves frayed almost to the breaking point. Dave treated her no differently than any of the others, a fact that troubled her. He was withdrawn, distant. They hadn't been together for more than a week—and her understanding nature was being pressed about as far as it could be. It was clear Dave was under a great deal of strain, and he couldn't—or wouldn't—let her help.

Gwen made certain that every item about the group

that appeared in the newspapers was clipped and pasted into the huge scrapbooks she faithfully kept for Dave. Many of the clippings contained praise for Ellen's talent. As Ellen read each review, her pride grew. She had worked long and hard for those words, and she relished them. She also longed for the glowing praise Dave had bestowed so liberally before. Working with him every day, singing romantic ballads, standing so close beside him, kept her emotions in a turmoil. She was relieved she had heard no more from Carl, and hoped she had succeeded in discouraging further contact. There was always the annoying idea in the back of her mind that he might show up again at any time. She wasn't certain if he had remained in Nashville after she turned him down. If Dave knew the answer, he kept it to himself. He didn't communicate with her as he had earlier.

Each time Dave brushed against her or touched her in passing, her body tingled with desire. Her arms ached to reach out to him, to hold him, to feel him against her again. She'd tried to talk to him but hadn't broken through, and was miserable at her failure. She was in love with Dave! And her love grew stronger and stronger with each passing day.

The weekend may have been restful for her body, but it was lonely and anguished for her heart.

Chapter Nine

DAVE USED STUDIO ONE, in the music-row section of
Nashville, to cut his eighth album. Ellen remembered
visiting the studio years earlier, when she and Carl had
been showing old friends around the city. It was small
and intimate, a place where many big stars had recorded
at one time in their careers. Stored within the soundproof
walls were the notes of thousands of songs sung by the
now-famous.

The sessions went well, and although everyone in the
group was tense, they all relaxed quickly as soon as they
were over. After the final session, laughing and joking,
they filed out into a late-afternoon rain. Dave waited in
the doorway for Ellen.

"Want to have some dinner?" he asked.

She looked up at him, blinking back windborne raindrops. "I'd like it a lot. Shall I follow you in my car?"

A slight smile tugged at the corners of his mouth. "No, let's play it the way we did once before. I'll have someone drive your car home. Here, toss me your keys. I'll only be a sec."

His words offered hope, and her heart beat faster as she waited for him to reemerge from the building.

Once settled in his Mercedes and on the road, Dave headed toward the outskirts of town. "I thought we'd go to the Jolly Ox, out in Murfreesboro. Ever been there?"

She shook her head. "I hear it's like a bit of old England, and I know they serve delicious crab legs and lobster."

He laughed. "Now you're talking my language. What do you say we tackle the bib and nutcracker and order the biggest lobsters in the tank?"

"I always feel like a murderer when I do that. I'll let you choose." Ellen relaxed against the seat, sighing. Dave's mood was a bit more upbeat than it had been lately. She supposed the recording session had been the source of a lot of the pressure he'd been under, and now that it was over, things could be much better between them.

Now and then, as he drove, he glanced at her. "You're sure making a name for yourself in a hurry," he said matter-of-factly. "Every day Gwen brings in another review where your name's mentioned. Have you had any big offers I don't know about?"

"No one has pounded on my door."

She was sure she heard him sigh and mutter, "They will. . . ."

Dave was silent then except for formalities, until they entered the restaurant, where he smiled at the hostess and gave his name, which didn't seem necessary because she returned his smile in the adoring way of the fan and led them to a corner table where a man was sipping a drink. He rose as they approached the table, and Ellen gasped, immediately recognizing him as the TV producer who made the offer of an appearance to her and Dave at Lenny's party. He extended his hand and she took it. But what was he doing here? She looked suspiciously at Dave.

"Hello again, Ellen. I'm pleased to see you here. Dave seemed quite sure you'd be interested in seeing me."

"Oh, he was?" She glanced at Dave who merely raised his brows. Annoyance shot through her. Obviously, she'd been set up. Dave had only asked her to dinner a few minutes ago and in a very casual way. How sure he was of his attractions! She pulled her thoughts back to the present.

"I'm afraid I don't understand all this, Mr. Springer."

"I phoned Dave late last night to tell him about a show I'm planning to tape here in Opryland pretty soon. I'm calling it 'Country-Music Future Stars.' It's a new idea I've had since I spoke to you two earlier about appearing together. For now I want to put that old idea on ice and do this future stars show. *And* I want to feature you, Ellen. How about it? I'd say your star is certainly on the rise."

Ellen glanced at Dave questioningly. He shrugged. "Don't look at me. This is strictly your move, Ellen. We haven't signed an exclusive contract, you know. You're still free to sing anywhere you want, after our shows, of course. When Tom called me about his idea, I told him I thought you might be interested and that I would arrange for you to meet him to talk about it." He raised his hand to hail a passing waitress. "Seven and seven for me, white wine for the lady and another Martini for my friend," he told the round-bodied young woman.

She nodded, staring first at Dave, then at Tom Springer, finally resting her gaze on Ellen's face. "Aren't you Ellen McKay...the singer with Dave Winston's group? I saw you on Grand Ole Opry...Oh, Miss McKay, you were wonderful...."

Ellen saw Dave square his shoulders, but it was impossible to read his expression. She shrugged off a sudden feeling of embarrassment. Dave had made the *choice* to wear dark glasses to keep his identity hidden, and she wasn't going to fail to enjoy her newfound recognition. "Thank you." She smiled graciously. "That's what I like to hear."

With a flustered giggle, the waitress moved off to fill their orders.

"Well"—Dave's voice was husky—"this is your night, for sure. How does it feel, having a TV producer after you and fans starting to recognize you? Your life is certainly changing, Ellen McKay. Can you handle it?" His smile seemed a bit cynical.

Ellen sighed, smiling at the two men. "I think so. I certainly plan to give it everything I've got! I just don't understand why you want to hide behind those glasses, Dave. I think it's exciting, having someone recognize you and actually know your name! I love it!"

Dave shook his head, looking amused. "That will change soon, Ellen. I guarantee it. Give yourself a few months, and you'll want to wear a beard, a gunnysack, anything so you can have a little peace and quiet."

The waitress brought the round of drinks and set them on the table, then she reached in her apron pocket for a slip of paper and a pen, which she handed to Ellen. "I have to ask for your autograph," she muttered. "I hope you don't mind. You're going to be famous, and I want to be sure I have your name in my collection. My name is Gayle," she informed Ellen.

Ellen's hand trembled slightly as she wrote on the slip of paper: "Best wishes to Gayle . . . Ellen McKay." Not very original but she would learn to be witty in time.

The three made small talk while sipping their drinks and enjoying their delicious but messy lobster dinners. Then, over coffee, Tom Springer again mentioned his TV offer. "What do you say, Ellen? I can mail you the contract in the morning, and we'll be in business. The deal is a good one—top money and plenty of publicity. We plan to do six shows to introduce special new talent to the American people, and we want you to be the country-music representative." He leaned across the table, his graying mustache twitching as he smiled at her. "How can you refuse the offer? You have nothing to lose, and a pocketful of money and hundreds of fans to gain."

She swallowed the lump in her throat. "What should I do, Dave?"

"I can't tell you what to do, Ellen. It's your career, your life. This is just one of many decisions you will have to face."

She drew in a deep breath. "I really think I should talk it over with my agent, Tom. I'll phone him later tonight."

Tom pushed back his chair. "Fine." He pulled a card from his suit pocket and handed it to her. "Have your agent phone me at my office tomorrow morning, and we can discuss your decision." He extended his hand to Dave. "Thanks for dinner, Dave."

When he left, Ellen sat staring at the flickering candles on the center of the table. Suddenly she felt tired, very drained, like a balloon that has lost most of its air. The evening had been a shock. Tom Springer's presence, as well as his offer, had come as a complete surprise. She had envisioned being alone with Dave. She glanced up to see a group of people at the next table staring in their direction. Dave's gaze followed hers.

"Looks like more of Nashville's supper crowd recognizes you, honey."

Honey. The word, which had once sounded flip coming from Dave's sensuous lips, then endearing, now had a coolly impersonal tone. Ellen felt suddenly alone. She shook her head. "I think it's you they recognize, boss."

The people whispered among themselves and continued to stare while Ellen lit a cigarette, took a long drag, then stubbed it out in a shallow glass ashtray and reached for her purse.

"Dave, let's get out of here."

His dark eyes twinkled in the candlelight. "Don't like being under the microscope, huh?" He reached into his pocket for his wallet and left a sizable tip beside his empty drink glass, then picked up the check. "It won't get better, but you'll get used to it."

She knew he was right, but at the moment the continuing stares unnerved her. As they walked past the table, she heard a woman whisper, "It is! That's the new singer...Ellen...Ellen something. Isn't she a pretty little thing? And *I'll* bet that's Dave Winston hiding behind those dark glasses," a man's coarse whisper exclaimed.

The rain had stopped, leaving puddles on the sidewalk and a light fog hanging dismally in the air.

"What now?" Dave's tone indicated indifference.

Ellen winced. How could she tell him that what she really wanted was for him to come back to her apartment with her, to take her in his arms and smother her from head to toe with his searing kisses, to set her body afire with a desire so tormenting that she'd beg him to go on . . . "Home for me," she said. "It's been a long day."

He spun the Mercedes around a sharp corner and gunned the motor, sending the car forward in a burst of screaming tires.

"Are you angry with me?" she asked. "If you are, I sure would like to know why."

She heard him give a little snort before he said, "Of course not. I just figured your life is heading the way you want it now, so we had better keep our heads clear and our hands off each other for a while. Think over Springer's offer. That could really light up the star on your dressing-room door. It's a good break."

His voice sounded bitter, and she reached over to touch his hand resting on the steering wheel, wrapping her fingers around his.

"You're different lately," she murmured.

He shook his head. "Not me, honey. *I'm* the same old Dave Winston, plodding to keep my place in line." He pulled his hand away. They were at her apartment building. He left the motor idling and merely reached across to open her door. "I'd better get out to Greyhound Acres. One of the bitches has pups due anytime. She had problems with her last litter, so I want to be there to hold her paw."

Crushed and confused by his cool dismissal, Ellen slid out the door. She stood at the curb, watching until Dave's tires spun dirt at the corner, their squeal breaking the silence of the evening. A strange, empty feeling gripped her.

Her agent assured her it would *certainly* be to her advantage to accept the offer to star on the first show of a new TV series.

"A chance like that doesn't happen to a newcomer

every day, El," he told her, and for once he didn't even mention money!

Mack was right, she knew. The breaks were coming her way. She asked him to go ahead with the deal and hung up, feeling almost high and very nervous. She paced up and down the small apartment, chain-smoking, and hating herself for it. In the smoky haze, the place began to look drearier than ever. There was a damp mustiness in the rooms, an old smell, stale cigarette smoke, foods cooked eons ago. She snatched the paper from the coffee table and sat down, folding it back at the want ads.

"Time to move onward and upward," she murmured as she scanned the "apartments for rent" page. The thought of moving gave her a sense of well-being, of taking a step toward improving her future. One ad caught her eye: "To sublet: large living room, bedroom, cozy kitchen and modern bath, completely furnished in beautiful early American." The address was Hendersonville. She got more and more excited. It was late, but she reached for the phone, her mind made up to a move as soon as possible.

The realtor answered on the tenth ring, sounding as if his sleep had been interrupted. Ellen felt a pang of guilt.

"I'm sorry to phone so late," she apologized. "This is Ellen McKay. I sing with Dave Winston's group. I just read your ad for the apartment in Hendersonville. . . . Yes . . . I'm very much interested." She nodded, listening to his reply and scribbling the address on an old envelope. "Yes, that's fine, Mr. Orson. I'll meet you there at eight in the morning. Thank you . . ."

Ellen spun around the room like a tightly wound top. Then, as suddenly as she had begun spinning, she stopped. Dave had called another early rehearsal to go over the road-tour music. He had a brand-new song he wanted them to try.

"Damn!" she muttered. "I can't miss seeing that apartment!"

She wondered if Dave had arrived home. With a shrug, she reached for the phone and dialed his number. Aggie answered, and after a few polite words, Ellen asked for Dave.

"He just came in the door," Aggie told her. "One minute . . ."

Ellen tapped her well-manicured finger on the table while she waited. Playing the guitar meant keeping her fingernails short, but she liked to use a natural pink polish. Her stomach felt jumpy when Dave answered. Aggie must have told him who was calling, because he put on a deep and sexy voice.

"So you just couldn't go to sleep without saying good night." There was a hint of sarcasm in his words. "I should have taken you in my arms under that street light and given you a proper good-night kiss. Do you want me to come back and help you relax?"

Something inside said: "Shout, 'yes' into the phone." Instead, remembering his recent coolness, she said, "Thanks, but no thanks, boss. I called to ask a favor of another kind."

His laugh was deep. "Well, you can't blame a man for trying."

She ignored the remark. "I wanted to ask if it would be all right if I come in a bit late tomorrow. There was an ad in the paper for a terrific-sounding apartment to sublet out in Hendersonville. If I can meet the realtor at eight, I'll have first crack at it. I have to get out of this place, Dave, and soon! You know what it's like; do you blame me for wanting to move?"

There was a long silence, and for a moment Ellen thought he might have hung up on or was about to refuse her request. Anger bubbled inside her, building up, ready to explode when and if he said no.

She heard him clear his throat before asking, "Just where is this place?" His tone held no warmth.

She told him the address and waited through another long silence. "Are you still there, Dave?" she asked him. "Do I get a few minutes extra in the morning, or not?"

She could almost see those magnificent broad shoulders of his shrug as he replied, "I suppose so. Just get here as soon as you can. We'll work around you."

Before she could voice her thanks, she heard him hang up the phone. Obviously he wanted no further conversation with her tonight, on that or any other subject. She sighed. Their relationship was cooling down to the freezing point. She felt a stab of suspicion. Maybe she'd completely misjudged Dave, and he wasn't all the warm and wonderful man she'd thought he was. He was behaving toward her very much like she was just a "sometime thing" with him. Could he really have enjoyed only the hunt, the conquest, and be interested in her now as merely a singer and an occasional bed partner? Yet another question came to mind: could he be smarting, really hurt even, by Tom Springer's zeroing in on her and waving away a TV appearance for him, too? She immediately dismissed the question. Dave was a big star. One television show couldn't mean all that much to him. She stewed about the answers—all bad—to her questions and cried herself to sleep.

Jed Orson was a mountain of a man who dressed in a custom-tailored suit and a corny, oversized Western hat. Ellen saw him standing in front of the apartment, on a quiet shady street in Hendersonville, leaning against his yellow Cadillac. He was talking to a woman, and when Ellen parked her car next to the curb and walked toward them, the woman turned and waved.

"Surprise, Ellen! I hope you don't mind my coming over to see the place, too." Gwen's smile was as warm as the early-morning air.

Ellen tossed her hair back over her shoulders, smiling. "I'm glad you came." She winked at Gwen. "I can use your advice, since I'm new at apartment hunting. At least, the elegant kind." She glanced up at the modern building with the solid glass front and tiny balconies overlooking the tree-lined street. It was certainly beautiful outside. Now, if the inside suited her *and* the rent was within her budget, everything would be perfect.

"We'll go right on in," Mr. Orson told them. "I'm sure you're going to be excited about this apartment, Miss McKay. Why, even the colors suit you."

"He does a terrific selling job, Ellen. He told me about it while we were waiting for you. It sounds perfect. You know, of course, that I'm here because my dear cousin called me last night and suggested I meet you." She shrugged. "Don't ask me why. There are times when I think I know him as well as I know myself; then again..." She shrugged again. "I guess he just didn't want you to get in over your head...."

"I didn't know he cared." Ellen managed a smile.

The elevator took them to the fourth floor, with Jed Orson talking nonstop about the fabulous new building and the superb apartments therein. He unlocked the door to 418 and stood back to let them enter.

"This is it, ladies," he announced. "Feast your eyes."

Ellen did just that. The room was like a layout from Beautiful Homes. Ellen's sandals disappeared into the thick green carpet as she walked to the oversized colonial sofa, which was upholstered in a bright, cheerful print of yellow, orange and brown flowers. A tall antique maple secretary stood between the windows on the far wall, and opposite was a large maple console TV.

"This is a palace!" she exclaimed. "Gwen, isn't it terrific!"

Gwen walked around the room, touching upholstery, running her slender fingers over shining wood, pausing in front of four Degas prints hanging on the wall above the davenport.

"I love it!" she exclaimed. "Ellen, it's *you!*" She turned to Mr. Orson. "This is a two-year sublet, right?"

He nodded. "The family that lives here is off on a round-the-world trip. We can rent the apartment for one year, with an option on the second. The rent is going to surprise you." He quoted a figure that made Ellen gulp.

"That isn't bad, Ellen," Gwen assured her. "If I were you, I'd snatch it up right now, before someone else does. I don't imagine it will remain empty very long."

Jed Orson shook his head in agreement, of course. "I'll have it rented by the end of the day."

Ellen sighed, walking across the room to the cozy kitchen, which boasted a microwave oven and modern, pastel-green appliances to complement the maple dinette furniture. She hurried to the sun-drenched bedroom to run her hand over the solid maple ball atop the bed post. "Isn't this a cannonball bed?" she asked the realtor.

He nodded. "Fine furniture it is, too. Fit for a king . . . or"—he smiled at her warmly—"a country-western singing star."

His words were a tonic to her ego. Mr. Orson was absolutely right. With stardom knocking at her door, it seemed only right that she have a *beautiful* door. She made up her mind quickly. "I'll take it, Mr. Orson."

Gwen, standing in the hallway peeking inside, smiled and gave her the A-OK sigh. "You're doing the right thing, El."

As soon as the lease was signed and she had written a check for the security deposit and first month's rent, Ellen scowled at her checkbook, shaking her head. "One thing is for sure—I'd better keep on climbing to the top. I certainly can't afford any backsliding."

Gwen laughed. "You don't have to worry about that. Dave said you're jet-propelled."

Ellen followed Gwen's car out to Greyhound Acres, and the two entered the studio together just as Dave called a break in the rehearsal.

He cast a glance toward the door, his dark eyes smoldering and unsmiling. "I had almost given you two up for lost. I thought I could count on you, Gwen. I sent you along to make sure we had a backup singer here at rehearsal before the day ended." He directed a scowl toward his cousin, who quickly vanished into her office retreat, wiggling her fingers at him by way of a reply.

"Did you get the apartment?" Janet Adams wanted to know.

Still seated at the piano, P.J. grinned at Ellen. "We placed bets . . . seven to one, saying you now have a ritzy pad where you can hang up your rhinestone-studded outfit. How about it? Are we right?"

Ellen glanced around the room at the group. In the short time she had been with them, they had become her friends. Only Dave had changed, and that change hurt her more than she could stand to think about.

"You said it was a seven-to-one bet?" she asked. "Who was the holdout?" Her eyes went to Dave's and held.

He winked one brown eye at her. "I was wrong, huh? You didn't turn it down, right?"

Ellen shook her head. "I couldn't. Oh, Dave, it's a dream. I plan to move in tonight, and just as soon as I'm settled, I want you all to come for an apartment-warming. How about it?"

Heads nodded and agreements were voiced. Ellen looked at Dave. "I haven't heard a reply from you, boss." She looked directly into his eyes, slowly blinking her own, her lips curved in a provocative smile.

"I'll be there," he said quietly. Then in an instant his mood changed. "You can all go on into the kitchen and ask Aggie to put on some coffee. Relax while Ellen and I go over the new song. As soon as we have it down pat, I'll call you and we can get on with rehearsal."

The group was glad for more time on the break. Tom and Janet walked arm-in-arm to the door, the others following, clowning it up with a whistled rendition of a song from Disney's *Snow White*.

Dave stood shaking his head, an amused smile on his face. "Crazy crew," he muttered. His fondness for his group was obvious to anyone who watched them perform. When the others had disappeared into the house, he turned to her, motioning toward the music stand.

"Shall we get to work? I want this one done with guitars . . . you play one verse, and I'll do the other. We'll do the third together." He picked up the guitar Red had left behind and handed it to Ellen. "Think you can handle it?"

Ellen felt herself stiffen at his tone. "I imagine so," she retorted, going over a few chords with fancy fingering to show him he needn't be concerned. He reached over to open the sheet of music on the stand and motioned her to begin. Ellen studied the page a moment, then began the introduction, playing through the first verse.

"OK, we'll sing the next verse," Dave told her. "Watch that timing... it's tricky in the fourth measure."

She nodded, keeping time with her foot as she and Dave played their duet. They sang several lines without a problem; then Ellen flubbed her fingering and had to stop singing.

"Damn!" Dave exclaimed. "That's just what I was afraid of. Keep your eyes on the music, Ellen... and put more feeling into the words. You sound like a robot in the spots where you *should* sound romantic." He put his guitar down and took Red's from her, laying it on the platform. She had a feeling something was about to happen, when he turned to her, taking her by the shoulders. "You do remember what it feels like to be romantic, don't you?"

She tried to pull back, but his hands tightened on her shoulders. "I just thought a little manhandling might help you get into the right mood to sing." He laughed. "Maybe a kiss might encourage you to sing with feeling." He pulled her close to him, his body hard against hers, and his mouth punishing hers with a searing kiss, his lips forcing hers apart. She struggled to pull away, but it was futile. His arms tightened around her.

"Damn it, Ellen...*feel!* I know you have a spark or two inside that gorgeous body of yours. I've sampled your passion. Remember? Put it into the song."

Anger seethed inside her, mixed with a yearning she couldn't deny. Her mouth felt bruised and swollen, and she fought the churning passion he had aroused. His next kiss was gentle, making her body shudder with desire. He released her, picking up the guitar and holding it out to her. "Now let's try it, shall we? Let's see if I've breathed real feeling into you, Ellen McKay...."

Tears smarted in her eyes. "How could you?" she gasped, fighting to remain calm. "I don't know what has been bothering you lately, or why you've changed toward me. But . . . I don't like it . . . and I'm not going to take it! I can't!" She turned, running almost blindly toward the door.

She heard him calling her name. "We have a lot of rehearsing to do. . . ."

Chapter Ten

WHEN GWEN OFFERED to help her move, Ellen was pleased, and invited her for a sandwich supper before they loaded their cars and headed for the new Hendersonville apartment. Ellen dressed in her old, faded jeans and pulled on a loose, man's shirt, an old one of Carl's she had borrowed years earlier and never returned to his closet. She pulled her copper hair back into a comfortable ponytail, then went to work before Gwen arrived, packing clothes, books and other items she intended to take to her new home. As she worked, she thought about the recent days and the upsetting turn of events at the rehearsal.

Dave had been almost cruel, and she could see no reason for his actions. She was sure of one thing. She had to leave the group. She hadn't meant her association with them to end as it had, but she could no longer work with Dave. If she stayed, being near him would be sheer torture. It was better to break all ties now and continue her career on her own. She had recovered from a badly broken heart once before; she could do it again. She wracked her brain to think of the exact time Dave had begun to change, and she thought of Carl's appearance in Nashville. That had to be the answer. Carl had been the cause of the change. . . . She couldn't let herself think ill of Dave's character.

Her belongings were packed, and the apartment as clean as her old vacuum could get it. It was ready to be shown and, she hoped, sublet until her lease expired, in three months. Mr. Orson had assured her he could find a tenant in no time, so she had left it in his hands. She combined tuna and hardboiled egg to make plump sandwiches and set a pot of cherry-almond tea aside to steep.

Gwen arrived a few minutes later.

"You should have worn work clothes," Ellen told her, eying her designer jeans and cashmere sweater.

Gwen's laugh was musical. "These *are* my work clothes. I do everything in jeans. I don't worry about the name on my hip. And the sweater can be cleaned—no problem."

"If you say so." Ellen laughed, nodding toward her tiny kitchen. "The food is ready, such as it is, so let's eat. I've packed everything I want to take to the new place, so I think that by using both your car and mine, we can probably make just one trip." While they ate, Ellen told Gwen about her decision to leave the group. No amount of persuasion could make her change her mind, and, reluctantly, Gwen seemed to accept it. She stayed at the new Hendersonville apartment long enough to help Ellen unpack some of her clothes and hang them in the closet, then glanced at her watch, moaning.

"I hate to leave you with so much still to unpack, hon, but I have to do my hair and nails before I turn in tonight. You know what a job it is to do long hair. There are going to be a couple of magazine reporters sitting in on rehearsal tomorrow, and I'll have to talk to them and fill in blank spaces for them. Dave hates to talk to reporters."

Ellen nodded, sighing. "So I'll miss a bit of publicity."

"Don't kid yourself." Gwen snorted. "They're going to want to know where you are, why you aren't there . . . everything. It will be interesting to hear what Dave tells them. He's going to *have* to answer those questions himself." She walked to the door, pausing with her hand on the doorknob. "Good luck."

Ellen nodded. "Let me know the results of the interview, will you?"

Gwen opened the door. "Sure . . . and don't worry. I'm *certain* Dave will take you back in a minute . . ."

Ellen shook her head. "Oh, Gwen, come on. Don't tease. It wasn't a firing or . . ." Her voice trailed off on notes of pain and emptiness. "Stop in anytime, Gwen . . . and thanks for your help."

The blonde nodded, and a wistful smile curved her lips. "Sure thing, friend. We'll keep in touch. You hang in there . . . and good luck on that Opryland TV show. I'll be sure to watch for it. You're going to be a superstar, Ellen McKay. Dave is right about that." She started down the thickly carpeted hallway, then turned back. "I'm sorry about my hardheaded cousin. You love him, don't you?"

Ellen leaned against the door, her knees feeling weak at Gwen's sudden inquiry. "Does it show?" she asked quietly.

"Let's say I've noticed a *few* signs." Gwen was clearly amused. "As I said, hang in there. Dave is really a great guy, but he can be stubborn as a hee-hawing Jenny, too. He and I have been close since we were kids, and I happen to know what he wants most in this world. It isn't fame—just a chance to play his music. And it isn't wealth—just enough money to be comfortable, and he's all ready got that. What he wants is the right woman to love and cherish, to make a real home and family. I thought for a while that he saw you in that dream, Ellen. I'll keep my fingers crossed."

"Don't!" she muttered, but Gwen was almost to the elevator, and Ellen decided not to call her back. What more was there to say, really?

Alone in the new world of the apartment, Ellen slumped on the sofa. The room, in spite of the familiar boxes now stacked in one corner, was fresh and clean, with furnishings she had dreamed of. Now this elegant place was home—but lonely and strange. She sighed, kicking off her shoes and curling up in the corner, surrounding herself with an array of plump, colorful pillows. She hugged one of them to her breasts. The beauty and warmth of the apartment was going to take a great deal of getting used to. She had told the members of Dave's group that she would give a party, and that was just what she intended to do. Dave could come or not. It was his choice. In a burst of anger, she made a fist and punched the fattest pillow on the sofa. Finding this gave her a feeling of relief, she pounded it again and again, until her tensions dissolved and she could lean back and survey her new kingdom with a sense of some inner peace.

Later she checked in with her agent, Mack, and learned the television deal was set. Her jubilation was marred only by the break with Dave. Hesitantly she mentioned it to Mack, whose silence revealed nothing of his reactions. Then, even more hesitantly, she asked him to tell Dave and work out any problems. But she expected none, she told him quickly, and was astonished by his curt response. Despite her success—which only benefited him, too—Mack sounded as cold to her suddenly as Dave was.

Ellen put her own special, personal touches on the apartment. The old Wedgwood vase that had been her grandmother's looked just right sitting on top of the big console TV. And the cut-glass bowl Carl's mother had given them as a wedding gift lent an added bit of elegance in its place of honor on the top shelf of the lovely corner curio cabinet. It was set next to a Hummel figurine, presented to her on her high-school graduation day by a favorite aunt. At the time, she'd been disappointed, preferring jewelry as gift, but later, as she matured, the figurine had become special to her. After her marriage to Carl, wanting to make their home comfortable yet elegant, she began to appreciate what she fondly called her "treasures." They were the only elegant things she had ever owned. Other bits of bric-à-brac were strictly from the discount store. But they helped to make the apartment more homey, more "hers." She set family photos on the tables and hung a needlepoint tapestry country scene she had made years ago on a blank wall in the bedroom.

The days that followed were busy with rehearsals for the upcoming TV special, but her conscience wouldn't let her enjoy the work anymore than her hurt feelings would. Finally, reluctantly, she decided to phone Dave. She couldn't stand the silence any longer. She waited until evening, when she wouldn't interrupt rehearsal. Expecting Aggie's voice, she was completely tongue-tied, for a moment, when he answered. His quiet voice had the same effect upon her as always, and she was tempted to hang up without uttering a word.

"Hey, anyone there?" he asked, after a long pause greeted his, "Hello, Dave Winston speaking."

The old tingle crept up Ellen's spine, igniting the embers that still smoldered inside her. She started to put the phone down, then shook her head and swallowed hard, trying to bring herself to speak. Dave's laugh rumbled into her ear.

"If this is one of my great army of fans wanting to hear my sweet voice, speak up. It makes a big difference who I'm talking to...a woman like Ellen McKay deserves a sexier greeting than the gal at the Pizza Port."

Ellen shook her head, grimacing. "How did you know it was me?"

He gave a short laugh. "There's a certain familiar sound to your silence, luv. After the way you dashed out that day, I figured it had to be you, calling to tell me you've come to your senses and asking if you can come back to the fold. Am I right?"

"Not exactly." Work...not feelings...was on his mind. Black anger rose in her. "I'm calling to say I think it's best this way. I know I shouldn't have run out and you could make things miserable for me in the future...but I want to go it on my own now, Dave. Actually, my days with the group would be numbered anyway. I'd be out of a job as soon as Lynn returned to work." Her voice was icy. "I just think you and I are like oil and water, and it's best if we stay miles apart. I only phoned because I wanted to tell you in person that I'm grateful for your help and encouragement, and for the chance to get my name in front of the public. I think I can handle my life now. I'm very grateful."

"How grateful?"

She couldn't tolerate the mockery in his voice. "Good-bye, Dave," she said evenly, and replaced the phone in the cradle, fighting back tears. The Dave Winston chapter in her life seemed to be ended now. Only the thought of the upcoming TV show, and the appearances it might lead to, kept her from sliding into a fit of tears and depression.

The ringing of the phone so soon after her talk with Dave startled her. She let it ring several times before picking it up.

"Hello..."

"Don't hang up, Ellen," Dave's voice told her. "Listen to what I have to say." His tone was serious this time, and Ellen sat back to hear him out. "The public isn't going to let us separate, you know. We're a duo now. We can't just give the music world a taste, then quit."

She bit her lip hard. He was right, but she had a feeling this might be his way of asking her to stay with his group, and she also wondered if it might be his own career he was thinking of. Dave was a star. He didn't need her or anyone else singing with him to keep him up on top of the charts.

A tiny wave of despair swept over her, and she shivered.

"I think all you want is a bed partner, Dave. And I want a career. I said it before—it just won't work with us."

There was a long pause; then he muttered bitterly, "Watch out, Ellen, your hat size is changing." And this time *he* hung up on *her*.

His last words stayed with her, returning at the most

inopportune moments during the next few days of rehearsals, interviews and costume fittings. Dave was wrong about her. Of course she liked being known, having make-up people transform her into a flawless beauty and cameras zero in for close-ups to be seen nationwide. It was an ego-booster when reporters snapped shots of her as she prepared for her TV filming. Anyone would enjoy what she was experiencing now. It seemed to her that she had worked an eternity for this chance to stand on her own. This show would be her own private moment of truth. Either her name would become a household word or she would slip back into anonymity. And besides, she knew—really knew now—that her career was her life. Men couldn't be trusted with emotions. And what was love, anyway?

The members of the television crew set up in Opryland early in the day to enable them to film before crowds of people intent on a day of fun swarmed through the gates. A few early arrivals were admitted to the park, to lend an air of authenticity to the background, but they were well informed about how to act during the filming. They were instructed to wander about the park with Ellen, to go on the rides and ham it up with the free-roaming animals in the petting-zoo area. Ellen went on some rides alone except for the camerman, who kept his lens on her as she mouthed the words to a new song, "I Have My Ups and Downs." Later, she'd dub the sound, matching her lips movements. She had never been fond of stomach-churning rides, and was terrified when the director insisted she climb aboard the Wabash Cannonball, a ride of severe corkscrew turns and loops guaranteed to weaken the strongest heart. To make matters worse, she flubbed it twice, screaming when she should have been mouthing the words of the song. The entire scene had to be shot again and again. Weak in the knees and stomach, she begged them to film her singing while riding on one of the small lake rafts next, to give her a chance to regain her composure. The television crew broke for lunch, and Ellen was surprised to see Gwen waiting for her on the sidelines.

"You look a bit pale, Ellen," she greeted her, smiling. "I think I would have fainted by now! *You*, my dear, are gutsy! How about lunch over at the Hamburger Pavilion? It's on me."

Ellen let her breath out in a sigh of relief. "I am so glad to see a friendly face! Believe me, this has been a morning I won't forget soon! I hope they don't have much footage to shoot after lunch, because I might not survive. The crowds are growing by the minute."

Even as she spoke, two teen-agers approached with cameras, to snap her picture, then quickly walk off, chattering about her bright spangled outfit and gorgeous hair. She and Gwen made their way to the eating place, and a line of people followed them.

"I feel like the Pied Piper," Ellen said, laughing. "Is this for real?"

"If it isn't, I'm asleep and having the same crazy dream. You have quite a 'following,' gal. Look, I hope you don't mind my showing up this way. I wasn't too busy, so I told Dave I'd like to come and watch your special being shot. Just because you and my dear cousin have severed your . . . relationship, is no reason you and I can't still be friends."

"You're absolutely right," Ellen agreed, matching Gwen's cover-girl smile. They reached the Hamburger Pavilion, ordered burgers and diet soft drinks and found a table where they could talk while they ate. Mostly they gossiped about the members of the group and steered far away from the subject of Dave.

The afternoon session was just as grueling as the morning one had been. Every bone in Ellen's body cried out for mercy. This time, Tom Springer suggested a change in the script. He wanted her dressed in a red-checked gingham dress and white Western hat, singing on stage of the rustic Folk Music Theater. The regular performers at the theater, a group of talented young people who imitated well-known performers, with the help of costumes, performed a clog dance behind her.

The filming ended with a scene on the old pastel carousel built out over the pond. For this, Ellen wore a Scarlet O'Hara type of gown and a wide-brimmed straw hat. When the shout, "It's a wrap-up" rang out over the noise of the many rides and the crowds wandering along the trails in the park, Ellen had the urge to find a quiet spot in the garden and curl up in the shade for a nap. Instead, she changed into her designer jeans and a pink striped blouse, and she and Gwen went to the Country Kettle for a hasty supper.

"I'd have asked you over to my place for something to eat, but I'm so tired I don't think I could even open a can of soup." Ellen managed a weak smile across the table. "I feel as if I haven't slept in a week. Who ever said singing was an easy way to make a living?" She eased her shoulders into a slump. Tom Springer chose that time to enter the restaurant and cross the room to their table.

He pecked her on the cheek. "Ellen, I'd say today's shooting was perfect. We got enough footage to make two shows. Do you think you could stand that?" His eyes crinkled at the corners in a smile, and she had the feeling her show make-up was melting into a glob and trickling down her face.

"If you mean it, Tom, I'm speechless."

He nodded. "I'll be in touch. If this show takes off the way I think it will, I just might try for a limited series . . . with you as star, of course. We can do segments at the Ryman, the Hall of Fame . . ." His enthusiasm was growing by the minute.

When he was gone, Ellen just sat there, pushing mashed potatoes and chicken gravy around on her plate. "Gwen . . . I'm certainly glad you're sitting here with me. I'm a dreamer, you know—I've been known to come up with some really terrific fantasies—but this one takes the blue ribbon!"

Gwen drained the last drop of coffee from the china mug as eagerly as she had devoured her plate of southern-fried chicken. "Oh, this is no dream. I heard Tom Springer with my own tiny pink ears. Wait until I tell Dave. I think he's been waiting to do a show at the Ryman for ages, but for some reason his manager never set it up."

Her words flashed like a warning in Ellen's mind. "Maybe you'd better not say anything until Tom's idea materializes. It could be just wishful thinking, after all. This show we filmed today might fall flat, and he won't want to do another show with me."

Gwen shook her blond head, scowling. "No doubts, Ellen."

"I'm just so afraid I'll do something wrong and this chance will zip out the window." She sighed. "It's hard to explain. I've wanted success for so long, and I've dreamed of money and fame, and the way my life might change. Now that it's in sight, I'm scared, Gwen. I'm afraid I won't measure up to everyone's expectations. I know that Dave and I sounded great together; I could feel it inside me. But alone"—she shrugged—"I'm not sure if I'm good enough . . ." Her voice trailed off.

She didn't see the woman coming up behind her,

holding a newspaper picture in her hand, until the bit of paper fluttered in her face. "You *are* Ellen McKay. I knew it! My husband said I was crazy, but I saw you sing on Grand Ole Opry, and I loved your voice. Besides"—she looked Ellen up and down, her eyes admiring her trim, jean-clad figure—"I loved your red outfit!" She wriggled her plump hips. "I sure wish I could wear one like it." She waved the picture again. "Would you mind signing this for me? I cut it out of the paper right after the Opry appearance, because I intend to buy your records."

Ellen took the clipping, signed her name across the bottom of the picture and handed it back to the woman, smiling. "Thanks for your kind words. I'll be featured on Dave Winston's new album, *Greyhound Tour*. And I hope I'll cut an album of my own one of these days. Keep your eyes open for it."

The woman nodded, obviously thrilled to be seen talking to such a glamorous person as Ellen McKay, and reluctantly backed off.

Gwen bowed her head. "I think I should pay homage, Your Majesty." Her smile turned to an amused giggle. "How does it feel to be recognized?"

"Now I know why Dave always puts on dark glasses in public places." Ellen's red lips curved in a smile. "Part of me craves the excitement of performing, of knowing I'm good and that people like to hear me sing, but...It isn't easy to have people stare at you, point and whisper when you come into a place. I had that on a smaller scale before, but it was different. Most of the customers in those honky-tonks were truck drivers and good-old-boy, red-neck types. All they wanted was a torchy song and a skimpy outfit. With me, they had to settle for tight jeans." She shook her head, sighing. "I'm glad that part of my career is over! I'll take my chances with whatever lies ahead."

The first in the series of television shows was aired just a month after filming. Ellen filled those days with interviews and fittings for clothes and by posing for pictures, going to small parties with people in the industry and having rehearsals at a private studio on Music Row. Tom Springer was convinced that once the Opryland taping was seen by the public, Ellen's would be a hit.

When the airing date was set, she invited the Greyhounds to her apartment to watch the show and to help her celebrate it's success—or drown her sorrows! Her invitation was delivered verbally by Gwen and included Dave. The other members of the group accepted readily, but Ellen wasn't surprised when she had no response from Dave. His total rejection and obvious disinterest really hurt, though she'd steeled herself for them. Somewhere, deep inside, she had hoped this evening might bring them back together, to at least a civilized, if cool, friendship.

Dave remained very much in her dreams. Awake, she could control her thoughts, keep them on safer ground, lose herself in her work. Asleep, Dave Winston was able to invade her mind constantly, manipulating it in a way that made her awaken with his name on her lips, wanting to feel the strength of his arms holding her, his mouth claiming hers in wonderful kisses. The dreams became *more* frequent, *more* real—not less so—as time passed.

Tom and Janet Adams, Sid and Alice Lewis, Joe Leone and his lovely wife, Betty, Red Martin and P.J. and his current playmate, Tam, a pencil-thin, six-foot, raven-haired lovely, arrived a short while before the Opryland show began.

"Chuck couldn't make it. Lynn picked tonight to go into labor," Janet told Ellen. "He'll watch your show at the hospital."

Gwen had come early to help make hors d'oeuvres, fill dishes with candy and mixed nuts and see that coasters were placed in strategic places to protect the expensive furniture from accidents. Everyone sat clustered around the king-sized TV, chattering, sipping drinks and nibbling the tiny sandwishes. When the opening music began and the camera panned across Opryland's many attractions, finally zooming in on a lone slender figure dressed in bright-red, form-fitting pants and a matching red shirt glistening with rhinestone trim, standing near the bubbling waterfall, the room went silent.

Ellen shivered at the sight of herself on the screen. It gave her a strange sensation, watching, hearing herself, remembering the endless rehearsals leading up to the TV special. She watched, mesmerized. Suddenly she knew the program made it . . . and that she was good. When the first commercial flashed on screen, those seated around the TV set began talking again, and glasses chattered as they were refilled at the small bar at the end of the room.

"You were terrific," Red exclaimed, adding ice to his whiskey sour.

"This show is going to get rave notices, Ellen . . . even from reviewers like Alf Thomas . . . and he'd pan his own mother on her birthday." Joe Leone reached for another sandwich as he spoke, handing one to his knicker-and-sweater-clad wife.

"Too bad Dave couldn't make it," Tom Adams said just before popping a small shrimp sandwich into his mouth.

"I think he had some last-minute details to go over

with his manager. There's going to be a big unveiling at the Wax Museum tomorrow," P.J. informed the group. "I happened to overhear part of the phone conversation." He shrugged. "I guess it's not something Dave wanted known."

His friend Tam giggled. "Maybe they put a wart on his nose or something."

The others ignored her remark. Ellen kept her eyes glued to the television screen, waiting for the commercials to end. The moment the Wabash Cannonball flashed on, Gwen raised her hand for silence. Ellen fingered the rim of her cocktail glass, reliving the wild ride, trying to put thoughts of Dave aside.

During the next commercial, after praising Ellen for her song on the frightening ride, the talk once again turned to Dave.

"He's been acting crazy lately. I think he's gone bonkers. He used to be fairly easy to work with, fun to be around." Red laughed. "If I didn't know better I'd say he was in love."

Ellen's breath caught in her throat.

Janet Adams lit a cigarette, using the sterling-silver lighter on the coffee table in front of her. "Well, if he is, he keeps her hidden. I've never seen him with a gal."

Those words sent a surge of relief through Ellen's body. She sighed, getting up to mix herself another, stronger screwdriver. "You people help yourselves, now," she shouted above the chatter, hoping to change the subject from Dave Winston.

When the last of the show's credits faded, Ellen switched off the TV and faced the applause and cheers of her friends. She bowed, smiling. Nothing could upset her at this moment. The show had been perfect, with no flaws, just fun and memorable songs. It was her evening to cherish, to remember in the days and years to come. Success had finally come to claim her, and it was like a wild, wonderful dream come true. She knew she owed tonight all to Dave.

"Thanks, gang, for sharing tonight with me." Her face was flushed from the cocktails and from the excitement of the television special. Her pride and satisfaction were marred only by Dave's not being there to share the good feelings.

The phone rang. As Ellen excused herself to pick it up, her friends filed out, waving and blowing kisses her way, muttering thanks and goodbyes, until only Gwen remained. She sat in the chaise longue, still looking glamorous in her frothy lavender gown, sipping her drink.

Ellen's smile widened more and more as she listened to the words being spoken in her ear. "Really, Tom?" She nodded. "Oh . . . I'm so pleased to hear that! Yes. I'll be anxious to hear the details. . . . Yes . . . Thank you, Tom. Good night." She put the receiver down and stared at it for a moment before turning to face Gwen. "It's a hit. Gwen, the sponsors are crazy about the show. They want me to do a series! Six shows!" She grinned, jumped to her feet, and yelped with joy. "Tom said the switchboard at the studio is lighting up like the White House tree on Christmas Eve. Pinch me, will you? I can't believe it. I'm really on my way up. I want to shout it out the window. 'Look at me—I'm Ellen McKay. I'm a *star*'!" Then her bubble burst. She sighed, suddenly looking very tired. "I wish I could share my feelings with Dave."

Gwen nodded. "I know . . . and I'm sure, deep down, he is hoping for this success for you. I'm going to drive out to Greyhound Acres as soon as I leave here. I want to corner my dear cousin and find out just what kept him away. I know he has the unveiling at the Wax Museum, but he has some other things cooking with his agent and his manager. His road tour starts next week." She put her glass down on the end table and stood up, tossing her blond hair over her shoulders. "I'll be sure he knows about your series, and I'll get back to you with his reaction. I'm on your side, remember. I might be prejudiced"—she winked at Ellen—"but I happen to think you and Dave belong together...singing and otherwise." She snatched up her white cape from the chair where she had tossed it on her arrival and headed for the door. "I won't tell you to relax and sleep tight. You're going to be flying high all night." She opened the door and turned to flutter a hand at Ellen.

"You just revel in it. Think about all of the gorgeous clothes you'll be able to buy now! No more borrowing from me." Her eyes crinkled at the corners in a teasing smile. "I just might turn the tables and borrow one of *your* Paris originals. 'Bye, now. I'll be phoning."

Ellen stood in the middle of her living room, hugging her arms to her chest and staring at the blank TV screen. Finally she sank down in a chair and switched on the radio, and country music filled the silence in the apartment. She leaned back to listen. When the announcer said, "Next, we are going to play a brand-new number sure to hit the top of the charts. It's called, 'We Need Each Other,' and it comes from Dave Winston's new *Greyhound Tour* album, which has just been released. This number features Dave and that lovely, auburn-haired songbird, Ellen McKay. Any of you folks out there who watched the 'Opryland Newcomer's Special' earlier tonight will be happy to know we're going to be playing this song featuring her a lot in days to come. Now, Dave and Ellen."

Tears stung Ellen's eyes as she listened to the softly blended notes of their duet drift into the room. She kept her eyes closed, trying to hold back the plump crystal teardrops that seeped out from under her lids and trickled down her cheeks. Her body seemed detached from reality, gently hovering in midair. Her thoughts were centered on Dave, and she fought the dreams invading her mind—dreams that seemed much too real, and that of course featured Dave.

She had no idea how long she had been asleep. The ringing phone awakened her, and she sat up, tossing the pillow aside and blinking back her overwhelming weariness. Dave's voice boomed into her ear, bringing her back to reality with a jolt.

"Ellen . . . I hate to phone this late, but I have a favor to ask. The Wax Museum is uncovering a statue tomorrow, and they want me there . . ." There was a long pause; then he added, ". . . with you beside me."

Ellen shook her head to clear the cobwebs. "Why me?"

"Publicity," he said simply. "Some sources believe we belong together, you know. Anyway, there will be photographers there. Will you come?"

"Sure," she said softly. "It might be kind of fun to see your wax twin. I have an early appointment, but I can work in the unveiling if it's in the afternoon."

"As a matter of fact, the unveiling is set for three o'clock on the button," he told her.

She nodded. "OK. Fine. I'll meet you at the Wax Museum at two-thirty . . . how's that?" The sound of his voice had started her emotional clock ticking again, and the thought of seeing him, even briefly, the next day made her want to sing.

"Thanks, Ellen." His voice was husky. "I hated to

ask, but you know how it is."

"Sure. No problem, Dave." She said good-night and hung up, wondering just what tomorrow might bring.

Chapter Eleven

GWEN HAD BEEN absolutely right about her having a sleepless night. Dave's phone call hadn't helped one bit. The satin sheets were cold ghosts stirring memories of Dave's warm arms. Ellen had set her alarm clock for eight, allowing just enough time to shower, dress in her new royal-blue flared skirt and white ruffled blouse, brush her hair until it looked like polished copper, apply her make-up and drive to her agent's office to discuss a contract for the TV series. After that, she barely had time to grab a sandwich, freshen up and head for the Wax Museum, keeping within the speed limit.

Dave was already waiting for her, seated in the parking lot in his Ferrari. She pulled into a spot close to the Museum. He eased his lean body out of the car and didn't even bother to lock his door before walking over to join her. Ellen bit her lip, her eyes unable to stray an inch from him. He looked especially appealing, in tan slacks, a light-yellow sport shirt and a brown-and-white checked jacket. Ellen took a deep breath, wondering if she would be able to get through the unveiling without giving way to her feelings for Dave.

"I still don't know why I had to come here," she said, smiling as he paused in front of her.

His broad shoulders shrugged, and he looked down at her, a wry smile tugging at the corners of his mouth. "I don't either, Ellen, but it was almost an order. I was told to phone you and ask you to come. The powers-that-be made it sound important—anyway, thanks."

She nodded, and they walked inside. They were early, but they didn't have to wait. They were immediately whisked into the interior, past rows of wax figures in glass cases. All the country music greats were there, from Stringbean and Grandpa Jones to Hank Snow and Loretta Lynn. Ellen and Dave stopped at a curtain-covered window, and the cameramen took prearranged places.

"What we want is for you two to go inside and stand with the figures..." the Museum director informed them.

Ellen glanced at Dave, whose expression was one of surprise. "How many are there?"

"Why...just two," the man said.

There was no time for conversation or protests. They were ushered around to the back of the case and helped inside, where two life-sized wax figures stood side by side, looking deeply into each other's eyes. The likenesses were uncanny. Dave's figure wore his familiar tan Western pants and black-spangled shirt and black hat, and he held his silver-trimmed guitar. Ellen's figure had on the bright-red outfit she had worn at the Opry, and, in her hands was a replica of her Sears guitar.

"Why didn't you tell me they had a wax figure of me, too?" Ellen whispered to Dave. "It's a shock to see myself standing here..."

Dave shoved his hat back on his head and scowled at the two wax figures. "I didn't know they had made one of you, Ellen. I swear. It's a surprise to me too." She looked up at him, sensing that he was less than pleased by the sight of their doubles.

"OK, you two, let's try a 'Which twin is the wax one?' scene. Move in close to your doubles; we'll use the same pose, without the guitars...." Rocky pushed Dave closer to Ellen, grinning. "Get with it, man. She won't bite, and this will hit the late-night papers, *if* we get it in on time."

Ellen and Dave dutifully posed for the flashing cameras, but Ellen could not look into Dave's dark eyes. They seemed all-knowing, probing, able to see deeply into her soul.

When the pictures had been taken and everyone in the dimly lit place returned to the sunlit lobby again, the reporters crowded close, firing questions at Ellen and Dave.

"Why haven't you two been singing together lately?" one short, mouse-faced woman shouted.

"Will you go on tour together?" a rotund, balding man wanted to know.

Dave raised his hand for quiet, and the entranceway became silent as the reporters obliged. "I'll answer those two questions... briefly." He took a deep breath before going on. "Ellen McKay is on her own now. We are no longer a team. And"—he glanced at Ellen briefly, unsmiling—"so, of course, we will *not* be going on tour together. Ellen came to work with the Greyhounds on a temporary basis, while one of my backup singers kept a date with the stork. That should answer your questions."

Next, a bespectacled, long-haired young man moved closer to Ellen. "How about it, Ellen? How does it feel to be a rising star?"

She flashed him a cover-girl smile. "I'm very excited about it, of course, but my name wouldn't be known if it weren't for Dave Winston."

Dave's masklike expression seemed to soften a bit, but his smile was not quite as warm as the ones she remembered before their relationship had become so painfully strained. Nevertheless, it warmed her entire body in that brief second, and she wanted with all of her heart to shout her love for him.

When the interview and picture-taking session had ended, Dave's smile faded, and suddenly Ellen felt as if she was with a complete stranger. Where once there had been a tender, wonderful closeness, there was now an atmosphere of chilly restraint. Ellen shivered.

"I'd better get back to my apartment," she murmured. "It was fun, especially since I certainly didn't expect to see myself recreated like that."

His shoulders seemed to hunch a bit, and he shook his head. "I guess you're just zooming into the limelight so fast they figured they might as well kill two singers with one ball of wax, so to speak." His smile was almost nonexistent. "I think it's time we had a talk, Ellen. So as long as we're both here and it's time to eat anyway, why don't we go out somewhere? There's a place on the corner . . ."

"Why not follow me to my apartment?" she suggested, surprising herself. "I might be able to come up with some scrambled eggs or something."

He shrugged. "Sure—why not?"

Ellen's eyes sparkled. "I *do* make a good omelette, honest. You look like you're afraid you'll starve. Worse, be poisoned!"

He reached out to take her arm in a strong grasp. "We're wasting time," he said, hurrying her out into the late-afternoon sun.

Dave seemed preoccupied as she set about preparing a light meal, beating the eggs and chopping bacon, mushrooms and onions. He watched her work silently, his expression unfathomable. His only remark was a surprised question.

"Tomato sauce?"

She laughed to cover her nervousness. "Sure. It's a trick I learned at my grandmother's knee. You'll like it, I promise."

He found beer in her refrigerator and poured it into two glasses while she dished up the omelette and set out a plate of muffins.

The omelette was good. Sipping cold beer, Ellen waited for Dave to speak up.

Finally he pushed his plate away and leaned back. The strain in the air was thick enough to snip with wire-cutters. And it was growing by the minute. Ellen felt a lump rising in her throat. Abruptly she rose and moved across the kitchen to stack their few dishes in the sink.

His chair squealed on the tile floor as he pushed it back and went to stand behind her. Ellen bit her lip, afraid to breathe as the scent of Dave's spicy after-shave reached her nostrils, and she felt her knees weaken at his nearness. She was suddenly shaken by her own need for him, as he reached out and turned her to face him. Electric shocks ran up her arms when his hands rested lightly on her shoulders.

"We have to talk," he said, but as he looked at her, his eyes took on a dreamy, bedroom look. In a second, his lips caressed her cheek, moving slowly down her neck to the deep hollow of her throat. His hands slid over her arms, then moved to her lower back, pulling her against him. She could feel his sudden need for her, and with a gasp she put her arms around his neck, letting her fingers lose themselves in his thick dark hair.

His smoldering eyes looked deeply into hers, and a faint smile tugged at the corners of his mouth. "To hell with talking," he whispered huskily. Once again his lips moved, this time finding hers to tease and tantalize.

"Oh, Dave..." she murmured, trembling with pleasure as his hands sought out the firm curves of her breasts. "I love you...I want you...please, Dave..." Her lips brushed his face, and she gently flicked her tongue across his mouth, loving the taste of him.

He took her hand and led her slowly and silently into her bedroom, where they stood for a moment in an embrace that set both of their bodies aflame. He gently eased her down onto the bed, his lean, hard body pressing against hers. One hand unbuttoned her ruffled blouse, pushing it back to expose her breasts. She knew now why she had chosen today to go braless. He stared at her a moment, his eyes betraying his emotions, then he leaned his head down to let his lips move slowly across the soft, perfect mounds, teasing her nipples into hard peaks. She felt her entire body respond, her desire mounting as he began to undress her slowly, letting each of them enjoy the moment, until she lay naked beside him, moaning.

"Oh, Dave..."

"You're beautiful," he whispered close to her ear.

She put a finger to his lips, shaking her head, then

reached out to unbutton his shirt.

He stood up, removing his own clothes slowly before he came to her, to lie beside her and let his arms encircle her and hold her close. Their lips met in a series of flaming kisses, with Dave's tongue probing her mouth and her own exploring his. The feeling of flesh against flesh, the wonderful hardness of his magnificent body pinning her to the bed, were all that mattered now. Heaven was such a small breath away as Dave's hands touched vulnerable places, making her body respond and arch against his as she moved with his caresses. Heaven descended, and Ellen shuddered with ecstasy.

When they parted they lay quietly. Ellen turned on her side, wanting to stay in the circle of Dave's arms. She let her fingers caress the dark hair curling on his chest. At her touch, Dave suddenly moved aside. Quickly he got up and retrieved his clothes from the chair near the bed.

His actions jolted Ellen. "What are you doing?" She sat up, clutching the satin sheets to her. "Dave . . . you can't leave now . . ." A bewildered, gnawing sense of rejection swept over her. Had Dave merely used her? Was it possible he hadn't felt as she had during their lovemaking?

"I have to get out of here," he told her, his tone unemotional, as if he were simply stating a fact. "Tonight shouldn't have happened, Ellen . . . I came here to talk to you . . . to get a few things straight. I don't know what made me lose control."

If he had swung his fist and hit her, she could not have been more hurt. His words cut deeply into her, and she pulled the covers higher, feeling suddenly very naked and ashamed. She had poured out her love to this man, given herself because she had wanted to, because she thought he loved her. Now he was once again the cool stranger of the past few weeks. Why was he toying with her emotions this way? "Dave, you owe me an explanation." She tried to keep her voice from quavering.

His back was to her as he pulled on his slacks and shirt, and he whirled to face her, zipping his pants with determined fingers. His face was clouded now by an angry frown. "Don't you know why? For starters, you ran out on me. We didn't have a legal contract, but our understanding should have been just as binding...and I should have been the one to terminate it." He glowered at her. "Our personal arrangement is over, too, no strings, no ties. And I don't think we should make any further appearances together...even if our managers and fans do think it's a good idea."

Ellen reached for her robe and slipped into it quietly, keeping her back to him until she had tied the belt. Then she slipped out of bed and crossed the room to stand in front of him. Her face was crimson as anger surged up in her, so much anger she couldn't even cry. She looked up at him in total disbelief. This was certainly not the Dave Winston she had fallen in love with...not the Dave Winston she had just made love with. This man with the cold, unfeeling eyes was a stranger bent on hurting her. She drew in a deep breath, squaring her shoulders.

"You're the one who asked me to come to the unveiling, remember?" she snapped. "I wouldn't have known about it if you hadn't called."

"The unveiling was news. Someone would have let you know," he growled. "I was 'advised' to call you...and it sure as hell proved to be a disaster. We should never have been paired like that, for everyone in Nashville to see. I'll get to work on it and try to have them separate us at the Museum. Actually"—his dark eyes narrowed as he looked at her—"I think they had a hell of a nerve making a figure of you. I've been in line for a spot in the Museum for a couple of years now." His jaw was set in a hard line. "Who did you have to snuggle up to?"

The tears finally came, slipping from her eyes to trickle down her cheeks. Sniffing, she bit her lip until it hurt. His words were like a sharp sword, cutting deeply into her heart. The veins in her neck showed her anger as the meaning of his words spun around in her mind. "How could you think such a thing? Get out, Dave . . . I don't want to ever see you again."

"You don't have to tell me to go. Remember the lyrics to 'The Gambler'? Well, I know when to hold 'em and fold 'em. And now I'm getting out of the game." He spun on his heels.

Moments later she heard the apartment door slam shut. She held on to the poster of the bed. Just a short time ago her world had been perfect, her future as bright as the evening star. Now she felt like she might collapse. What had made Dave turn on her with such venom? She put her fingers to her lips, still puffed and throbbing from their passionate kisses. And suddenly it hit her: Dave felt threatened by her sudden rise! The idea seemed crazy but true. Her success was tormenting him. She was sure of it!

Ellen hurried to her desk to answer the telephone.

"El, just a quick call to congratulate you," Carl's deep voice boomed into the phone. "I saw your Opryland special, and it was great! The offers are going to be pouring in now. Listen to a word of advice from one who knows . . . choose carefully."

Ellen sighed, not really wanting advice at the moment—from anyone. "Thanks, Carl...I'll remember. How are things?"

He laughed. "Not bad...I'm doing fine, here in Phoenix. This gig has been extended for a month, so I'll be eating for a while at least."

"I'm sure you'll do OK," she told him, barely hearing his words.

His voice droned in her ear. "Yeh, I'm trying to stay in the running. I'm cutting a new record next month in Bakersfield." There was a long pause; then he continued, his voice almost a whisper, "Hang in there, El. You can handle it...." With those words, he hung up.

Ellen replaced the phone on the cradle, sighing. It was decent of Carl to let her know he liked her show; at least now they could speak civilly to each other. Carl was a part of her past that she had wanted desperately to forget, but she knew now that past was a part of her and *always* would remain with her. Maybe in time both she and Carl would find happiness with others, and the dreams and hopes they had shared early in their marriage would yield better results.

She gave a bitter laugh. That dreamed-about happiness had eluded her again tonight. It would take a lot of willpower, probably more than she had, but she would *try* to forget that tonight had ever happened.

Busy days of rehearsals, costume fittings, interviews, and meetings with her manager and producer gave way to long, lonely nights. It wasn't easy to push thoughts of Dave aside. He haunted her during every lonely moment.

Tom Springer invited her to dinner one evening, after a strenuous rehearsal, and the change of pace was the boost her sagging morale needed—for a short time, at least. Tom was pleasant to be with, a widower with grown children, and she was pleased to receive the dozen lovely crimson roses delivered to her door the morning after their date.

Gwen had gone along on the Greyhound tour, and her daily phone calls kept Ellen up-to-date on the happenings on the road. Nashville seemed as empty as her feelings were bruised and battered. Part of the beating came from the local radio stations, which gave a great deal of air time to the new *Tour* album. Even though hearing the music she and Dave had made together was like salt on her wounded heart, Ellen could not turn the dial to another station. She listened, and she suffered.

Her agent phoned with the news that she had been selected as a presenter at the special Fans' Country Awards, to take place in one short week. The event would be taped for broadcast later as a special. Ellen was elated at the chance for the exposure. It was another of her dreams come true, and one that had come as a complete surprise.

With her career in high gear, magazines demanded picture layouts and interviews. Her days were filled, but she was kept informed about the Greyhound tour through Gwen, and shared her friend's excitement when she described Chuck and Lynn's small wedding, between performances, in a chapel in Buffalo, during the last week of the tour.

That same night, Ellen was reading in bed. The words on the pages began to blur, and she fought sleep, trying to finish the book before turning off the radio and light for the night. The announcer's urgent voice didn't penetrate her mind at first; then a name he spoke made her put the book down with a start.

"Dave Winston was injured in the crash. At this time, the extent of his injuries isn't known. We will keep you posted as we hear more news...."

A numbing chill swept over Ellen, followed by a feeling of great helplessness. Dave was hurt! Where? What had happened? She had to know! She slipped out of bed, putting on slippers and robe. Certainly Gwen would know.

She stumbled over the throw rug in her haste to reach the phone. The cold, clammy feeling engulfed her entire body now as she checked the Greyhounds' itinerary and tried to dial Gwen's hotel number. Her trembling fingers slipped, and she redialed, tapping her foot nervously as she counted the rings.

"Come on, Gwen...be there..." she begged. On the tenth ring she hung up, biting her lip and tasting her own salty tears as they streamed down her face. She sat down at the desk, lighting a cigarette before dialing Greyhound Acres. Aggie would probably have been called by now, she reasoned. Aggie's raspy voice answered on the sixth ring, and Ellen quickly put out her cigarette in the glass ashtray on the desk.

"Aggie, this is Ellen. I heard about Dave on the radio. Please tell me...what happened? Is he all right?"

"I don't know too many details," Aggie told her. "The hospital in Rochester phoned me a little over an hour ago. It seems the bus was in an accident. A semitrailer jackknifed on the rainy expressway and skidded into the front end of the bus. For some reason, Dave was driving—I don't know what happened to Bill or why he wasn't at the wheel as usual."

Ellen rocked back and forth to help curb her impatience. "Aggie...did they say how badly Dave is hurt?"

There was a long pause at the end of the line, and

finally Aggie's voice echoed in Ellen's ear. "As soon as Gwen finds out anything, she's going to phone. I'll let you know."

Ellen slowly moved to the bed, where she and Dave had made love, where their bodies had blended so perfectly into one. Every moment she and Dave had shared flashed in review. The love she had tried to keep buried under feelings of resentment and anger rushed to the surface as she made a hasty decision. There must be a late flight to Rochester. She would be on it. She could not satisfy her anxiety with phone calls. The man she loved was lying in a hospital bed in a strange city, and she wanted to be there, to see for herself the extent of his injuries.

She phoned the airline; then, after making a reservation on the late-night flight, she pulled her carry-on suitcase out of the closet and packed a few items of clothing and make-up. She showered and dressed in her new lilac Western-design pants suit, pulling her hair back and holding it in place with a lavender ribbon. She checked her wallet for money, crammed her checkbook into her shoulder bag and, before heading for the airport, called Aggie with her plans, then put in a call to her agent.

Ellen had plenty of time to think while waiting for her flight, which was late in leaving. Her thoughts continued while winging her way to Rochester, a city built on the picturesque Genesee River, near the shores of Lake Ontario. She took a cab from the airport directly to Strong Memorial Hospital, where Dave was being treated. Gwen was in the waiting room when she arrived, and hurried to meet her as she stepped off the elevator.

"I tried to phone you," she told Ellen. "I called Aggie, and she said you were on your way here." She motioned to the waiting room, and they went in to sit down. The room was empty except for a middle-aged man dozing in his chair, an open magazine draped over his knees.

"How is Dave?" Ellen hurriedly lit a cigarette and inhaled, waiting for Gwen's reply.

Gwen looked tired as she spoke. "He drifts in and out of consciousness. The doctor said that's common with a head injury."

"Common but not good." Ellen shook her head. "I want to see him. . . ."

"He might not even know you're there," Gwen warned, "and he looks dreadfully pale. . . ." She shivered. "I've never seen Dave like that. He always seems to have such a wonderful color . . . as if he's been on the beach in Bermuda for weeks. How could that color fade so quickly?"

"I came to see him, and I'm going to. Which room is he in, Gwen?"

Gwen sighed. "The end of the hall, last door on the right . . . do you want me to come with you?"

"No." Ellen shook her head. "I want to go in alone."

Her heels clicked as she walked along the shiny hallway. A blue-uniformed aide ambled along in front of her, pushing a cart laden with glasses of orange and apple juice. She stopped at the next room, and Ellen hurried around the cart, almost colliding with a white-coated lab technician who gave her a toothy smile and muttered, "Oops," as he went on by.

Dave was alone in the room, with a monitor beside his bed beeping his vital signs to the nurses stationed in the hall, in case of any significant changes. Ellen stood halfway inside the room, staring at the inert form stretched on the bed. The iron sides were pulled up, and a white bandage encircled Dave's forehead like a headband. She moved closer to the bed, pulling up a chair and sitting. Gwen was right. Dave was as white as death, and as quiet. A helpless feeling engulfed her, and she bit her lip and she reached out to touch his hand. There were wires attached to places on his body, and an intravenous tube dripped a solution from an overhead bottle into his outstretched arm. The sheet was pulled partway up his chest, but the fringe of dark curly hair was exposed. The flicker of a smile moved Ellen's trembling lips as she ran her fingers over it gently, blinking fast to keep tears from clouding her vision.

"Dave," she whispered, "I'm so sorry this happened. . . ."

His eyes remained closed, and although there was no sign that he had heard her, she thought for an instant she had seen his eyelids move slightly. She sat quietly, watching the beeping monitor and searching his face for any sign of awareness. A plump, middle-aged nurse padded quietly into the room.

"He is such a handsome man," she whispered. "I'm a big fan of his." She giggled and looked harder at Ellen's face. "Why, aren't you Ellen McKay?" she asked finally.

Ellen sighed, letting the tiny smile grow a bit. "There are times lately when I'm not sure who I am."

The nurse chuckled. "I'm so pleased to see you in person . . . I saw you on TV."

Ellen nodded, not feeling up to talking about her career at the moment, not with Dave lying there looking so ill. She knew the nurse wanted a personal word, and she forced a bigger smile. "Thank you . . . that's what I like to hear."

The woman reached out to pat Ellen's hand. "Don't you worry about Mr. Winston. He's going to be just fine after a few days of rest."

The nurse left, and Ellen turned her attention back to Dave. She leaned over, letting her lips touch his cheek in a gentle kiss. "I love you," she murmured in his ear.

His eyes flickered open, and he looked straight at her. "Do you?" His voice was a husky whisper.

Ellen moved back, startled. "You've been listening all this time! You knew I was here! Dave Winston, you are impossible."

"Make up your mind. Do you love me or hate me?" His tone was sarcastic. "Why did you come all this way, anyway? Don't tell me you just happened to be in the neighborhood. I know for a fact you have plenty to keep you busy in Nashville these days."

She jumped up, her hands on her slim hips, and glared down at him. "I came to see if I could help you out. I heard you won't be able to make your last shows. Gwen said they're having trouble finding someone to fill in for you. I came to volunteer."

"Wouldn't that cut into your busy schedule?" He looked up at her with expressionless eyes. "You're on a roll now, honey; I couldn't cut into that." He closed his eyes, and she could almost hear him sigh. The monitor beside him beeped faster, and she glanced at it nervously.

"Dave . . . please, don't talk like that . . ." Her voice was quiet and pleading. "I came because I care. . . ."

He turned his face toward the wall. "Sorry you made the trip for nothing. I'm getting Lenny to take over the show for me. So just hop the next jet back to Music City and get on with your career. . . ."

"Why do you do this to me, Dave?" She choked back tears.

"Just go on home, Ellen. I'm sorry you made the trip for nothing." He sighed. "Look, I'm tired. They told me to get some sleep, so I'd better do just that."

She backed toward the door. If it hadn't been clear before, it was now. It was over between her and Dave. Any feelings he had had for her were definitely gone. The sterile, antiseptic-smelling room began to close in on her. She felt as if her insides had been scooped out, leaving her more empty than she had ever been. She'd go back to Nashville, all right, and fill her days and nights with appearances and hard work, and not a single thought of Dave Winston! That was a promise she would once again make to herself—and this time keep.

Chapter Twelve

THE FANS' AWARDS were scheduled for the ballroom of the lovely, sprawling Opryland Hotel. Ellen concentrated on that event, going so far as to have a special gown made for her appearance as one of the presenters. Everyone important would attend the event.

The evening was sprinkled with stardust and glitter. In the dressing room, Ellen put on her new, flowing chiffon gown, brushed her auburn hair until it shone like burnished copper as it cascaded over her shoulders, dabbed on eye shadow and pink lipstick and stood back to look at the results in the dressing-table mirror. She heard the door open and whirled around, startled.

"Gorgeous." Gwen's voice came from the doorway. "Hope I didn't scare you."

"Oh, no. I've had coronaries before!" Ellen laughed.

"It's good to see you again. I've been so busy with shows, I haven't even had a chance to phone. I'm glad you came. Is Sam with you?"

Gwen, looking beautiful in a form-fitting yellow satin gown, with her hair newly tinted a lighter shade of blond, nodded. "Sure. Where I go, Sam goes . . . and vice versa. One of these days I'm going to say yes and marry the guy. I don't think I'll find anyone I'm more compatible with." She scowled slightly. "But what you really wanted to know is if Dave is here tonight. Right?"

Ellen sighed, dabbing at her nose with a powder puff, and looked at Gwen in the mirror. "How is he?"

"Great. The headaches are few and far between now, so I'd say he's on the mend. Actually, that's why I came here to see you . . . about my dear cousin. He's out in the audience tonight, but he wanted to keep a low profile so you wouldn't get upset."

"Upset? Why should I? I'm beyond that now, with Dave. He slapped me down pretty hard when I went to see him in the hospital. I can take a hint when it's hammered home to me hard enough and long enough. I just thought since we are"—she shook her head, closing her eyes a moment—"*were* friends, I should offer to help him out with his commitment. He made it very obvious he wanted no part of it."

Gwen eased herself into one of the plump chairs in the room. "He's just bullheaded. I know for a fact he was really touched by your offer." She opened her beaded purse and took out a crimson lipstick, putting it on her full mouth.

Ellen's laugh was bitter. "I find that hard to believe. No, Gwen, your cousin and I will have to stay at least a mile apart to get along. Heaven help us if we're even in the same room."

A warning buzzer sounded, and Gwen stood up,

shrugging. "Well, I tried. Now I'd better join Sam at the table. It sounds as if things are about to start. Are you singing tonight, or just giving out one of the awards?"

Ellen smiled. "I have a spot at the end of the show. I'll do one number, that's it. And I'll be giving the Fans' Award for the Best Single of the Year. I'll probably see you after the show . . . but please . . . just you and Sam."

The awards given were unique, designed to look like a bent record set on a crystal base, with the name of the artist and award earned engraved on the record label. The event was extremely glamorous and very formal, with the stars in the audience seated at round tables, dressed in their most colorful outfits. When Ellen's turn came to give the award, she came on stage unprepared for the applause that greeted her, and stood behind the small podium, facing the audience, her knees shaking and tears of happiness teasing the corners of her eyes. The applause in the banquet room came from her peers, and it warmed her heart. To have them appreciate her music made the struggle for success worthwhile. She let her eyes wander over the audience, finally pausing at the table where Gwen and Sam were sitting. Dave was there too, looking handsomer than ever, in a blue custom-tailored Western suit and white ruffled shirt. His eyes seemed to cover the distance between them and bore into her, and when the award envelope was handed to her, her fingers trembled as she tore open one end to remove the paper inside. Her mouth felt dry, and she swallowed before glancing again at the audience, avoiding the table just off center from which Dave was watching.

"The Fans' Award for the Best Single of the Year goes to Lenny Burton for that hauntingly beautiful song of his, 'Heartache Mansion.'"

Lenny, seated at a front table, stood up amid loud

applause and made his way to the stage, where Ellen handed him the record award and gave him her prettiest smile. "Congratulations, Lenny," she told him.

He took the award and planted a kiss on Ellen's cheek. "Thanks, beautiful," he murmured; then, in an even quieter voice, meant for her ears alone, he added, "Old Dave is suffering out there, you know. Talk to him." He turned to wave the award over his head and flashed a toothy grin at the audience. "I'm sure glad the fans think I deserve this. I'll put it on my mantel, where I can enjoy looking at it."

With the presentation over, Ellen went backstage, joining others to listen to the rest of the awards. When guitarist Tony Smith announced the Duo of the Year Award, a hush fell over the banquet room. Ellen felt a churning of anticipation in the pit of her stomach. Up until this moment she had not given any thought to the possibility that she and Dave might win an award for their duets. When their names were announced, her entire body seemed to go numb. Someone standing behind her gave her a gentle shove toward the stage, and she squared her shoulders as she walked into the spotlight, head high, her gown moving like the soft wings of a lovely Luna moth. The audience was clapping, whistling and shouting when Dave bounded up onto the stage to take his place beside her. He looked down at her and winked.

"Well, here we are..." he said lightly. "We can't seem to stay away from each other, can we?"

The presenter gave them each an award, and Ellen took a deep breath before acknowledging the honor. "Thank you. This is my first award, and I'm thrilled and grateful. I owe it all to this man standing next to me."

Dave kept his eyes riveted on the audience. "This little gal offered to give up a lot of appearances to fill in for me on the last shows on my road tour. I guess you all know I was involved in a fender bender, head banger. I think she deserves all the credit for this award . . . and many other things."

The applause kept on until Dave went back to his table. Ellen again disappeared backstage, until it was time for her song. Then she sat perched on a stool in center stage, her shiny new guitar around her neck. She strummed quietly, singing a song written especially for her by a new songwriter in town, a song she thought had potential, one she wanted to help become a hit. It was a ballad, a gentle story of a country girl and a city boy who fall in love, part, find new love, then meet again to find their love has never dimmed. The applause was enthusiastic, and Ellen felt tears of happiness trickle down her cheeks. It was an evening she would never forget, and henceforth it would be known as the evening she finally "arrived" in Music City, U.S.A.

When the show ended, Ellen hurried to her room, to relax and think over the events of the evening. The room boasted a velvet chaise longue, which looked very inviting to her weary bones. Just as she leaned back, carefully spreading the yards of material around her, a knock on the door broke the peaceful quiet.

"Who is it?" she called, her voice almost a sigh.

"It's me, Ellen . . . Dave . . ."

A frown creased her forehead, and for a brief instant, she wanted to tell him to go away and leave her alone. But there was still a part of her that hoped, and with a trembling sigh she called out, "Come on in . . ."

He stepped inside, closing the door and leaning against it. "I made a reservation for two at a new dine-and-dance place out near Brentwood, Ellen. How about it? Just for old times' sake...to celebrate our award?" The velvet eyes bored into her. "And to talk," he added.

There was no way she could say no.

The went in Dave's Mercedes, neither of them talking as they drove across town and headed into the sprawling suburbs. When Dave pulled into a blacktop parking lot, Ellen glanced out the window to see a long, rustic building built of white stone and dark wooden beams. Its name, The Gemstone, was flashing in bright neon.

"This place just opened," Dave said. "I thought we might do our celebrating out here in a private room, away from the usual hassles."

She nodded, understanding now the hazards and tribulations of fame. But once in the small private dining room, where a fire blazed cozily in a stone fireplace, warming every corner and bathing the pine-paneled room in soft light, her doubts surfaced to plague her. It was one thing to be with Dave in a crowded restaurant, and still another to be here in this cozy, intimate room. At the moment, she wasn't at all certain she could handle it, especially when he took her by the hand and led her over to a loveseat in front of the fire. "Let's sit down here and wait for the waiter to bring our dinner. I hope you won't mind that I ordered earlier."

She glanced at him, surprised. "How did you know I'd even come here with you?"

His smile was eye-twinkling, the kind she couldn't resist. "I think I know you pretty well, Ellen McKay."

They sat down, and very slowly and deliberately his arm slipped around her shoulders. He leaned close, letting his lips brush against her silken hair and move to the warm softness of her cheek. She jerked away and pulled back to stare questioningly into his eyes.

"I don't know how I could have been so wrong,

honey," he said huskily, the last word once again a term of endearment. "I've had a big problem, you know, and I've been sick over the rotten way I've treated you lately. I love you, Ellen, and I have for a long time, but I was afraid of your drive for success. Then I was afraid of your real success and how it would affect you *and* me. Now I know. I need you. We need each other. We're a very special team . . . now and forever."

He sighed. "Jealousy! That's what it amounted to. Isn't that crazy? Here I am, a grown man, supposedly intelligent, and I'm jealous of your shooting ahead so fast, doing things I've always wanted to do." He shook his head, laughing, and tightened his arm around her. "I wanted to film a show at Opryland, but Rocky was never able to get a rise out of them. And I wanted to do a special at the old Ryman, too. Even the big unveiling at the Wax Museum turned me an odd shade of green. I'm not proud of the fact, but I thought it was the great Dave Winston they wanted to display in life-sized wax. I freaked out when I saw that gorgeous double of you beside me. Damn! I've been a fool, with a capital letter, Ellen." His hand tightened on her shoulder. "I accused you of having a big head! Heck, I'm the one whose hatband expanded a couple of sizes. I was suspicious as hell, too. Thought you were using me. Thought you didn't have any real love to give this lowly country singer, Ellen McKay. And I almost blew it all, didn't I? Thank the Lord you came to Rochester when I was flat on my back in that hospital bed. I knew then just how important you are to me. You would have given up so much to help me out. That told me something I should have known all along. We can work together or apart."

Ellen was spellbound by his confessions. And suddenly, she knew she, too, had some to make. "I was too proud and too ambitious . . . and too scared of trusting and then being hurt again. And I was insensitive to your feelings, Dave. I remember when I was a jealous person. It hurts, my love. I know."

A faint smile curved Dave's sensuous mouth. "Did you hear what I told you, honey? I believe I mentioned that I love you. How about it——do you think you can forgive this suspicious, green-eyed monster?"

She leaned closer, unblinking as she looked at him. "Why, Dave, I don't know what you mean. You have the warmest brown eyes I have ever seen. . . ."

He laughed, letting his lips brush across her. "You're a helluva woman. I've done a lot of thinking since I cracked this hard head of mine. I guess that accident was good for me. The next tour is slated for six months from now, and it'll cover the West. Let's go as a team. As Mr. and Mrs."

Ellen reached up and held his cheeks between her palms. She pulled his head down to hers and kissed him deeply.

He nibbled playfully at her ear. "Just think," he said huskily, "we can make love in Houston, Phoenix, Denver, and in every other city we play . . ."

She nestled comfortably in his arms as he held her close. "Do we have to wait that long?" she whispered, her heart throbbing hard against his. This moment was like the tag line to a ballad titled, "The Happiness of Ellen McKay."

"Heck, no," he murmured against her hair. "How about spending forever at Greyhound Acres, starting tonight?"

The flames erupted, full-blown and all-consuming. Ellen moved slowly in his arms in a way designed to make him release all stops. She was at home in those strong arms, at home, where she belonged forever. Her marriage to Carl had been merely a youthful mistake, the feelings totally unlike those she experienced with Dave. Her doubts and fears went up in the consuming flames, and she returned Dave's kisses hungrily, every part of her body responding. Only after several minutes did she pull back long enough to laugh happily.

"Does that answer your question, Mr. Winston?" Her eyes sparkled with love, and once again she moved close, letting her throbbing lips part for his kisses.

There was a faint knocking on the door, and a man's voice called, "Waiter..."

Dave reluctantly raised his now-tousled head long enough to answer, "We're not hungry!"

Ellen stirred in Dave's arms, her world complete. "Not for food, anyway." She chuckled.

And there were no further knocks to disturb them.

QUESTIONNAIRE

1. How many romances do you *read* each month? _____

2. How many of these do you *buy* each month? _____

3. Do you read primarily
   - ☐ novels in romance lines like SECOND CHANCE AT LOVE
   - ☐ historical romances
   - ☐ bestselling contemporary romances
   - ☐ other _____

4. Were the love scenes in this novel (this is book # _____)
   - ☐ too explicit
   - ☐ not explicit enough
   - ☐ tastefully handled

5. On what basis do you make your decision to buy a romance?
   - ☐ friend's recommendation
   - ☐ bookseller's recommendation
   - ☐ art on the front cover
   - ☐ description of the plot on the back cover
   - ☐ author
   - ☐ other _____

6. Where did you buy this book?
   - ☐ chain store (drug, department, etc.)
   - ☐ bookstore
   - ☐ supermarket
   - ☐ other _____

7. Mind telling your age?
   - ☐ under 18
   - ☐ 18 to 30
   - ☐ 31 to 45
   - ☐ over 45

8. How many SECOND CHANCE AT LOVE novels have you read?
   - ☐ this is the first
   - ☐ some (give number, please _____)

9. How do you rate SECOND CHANCE AT LOVE vs. competing lines?
   - ☐ poor
   - ☐ fair
   - ☐ good
   - ☐ excellent

10. Check here if you would like to
    - ☐ receive the SECOND CHANCE AT LOVE Newsletter

....

Fill-in your name and address below:

name:_____

street address:_____

city_____ state_____ zip_____

Please share your other ideas about romances with us on an additional sheet and attach it securely to this questionnaire.

PLEASE RETURN THIS QUESTIONNAIRE TO:
SECOND CHANCE AT LOVE, THE BERKLEY/JOVE PUBLISHING GROUP
200 Madison Avenue, New York, New York 10016